# Sweet Home

# Sweet Home

Wendy Erskine

Stories

PICADOR

First published 2018 by The Stinging Fly Press, Dublin

First published in the UK 2019 by Picador
an imprint of Pan Macmillan
20 New Wharf Road, London N1 9RR
Associated companies throughout the world
www.panmacmillan.com

ISBN 978-1-5290-1706-9

Earlier versions of some of these stories appeared in *The Stinging Fly*
(issues 34, 36 & 38, Volume Two), in *Stinging Fly Stories* (2018), and in *Female Lines:
New Writing by Women from Northern Ireland* (New Island Books, 2017).

135798642

A CIP catalogue record for this book is available from the British Library.

Printed and bound by CPI Group (UK) Ltd, Croydon, CR0 4YY

# Contents

I remember a house where all were good

　　To me, God knows, deserving no such thing:

　　Comforting smell breathed at very entering,

Fetched fresh, as I suppose, off some sweet wood.

—Gerard Manley Hopkins, 'In the Valley of the Elwy'

# To All Their Dues

## Mo

Three types of beauty salon: the pristine Swiss clinic set-up where the staff might as well be in scrubs; tart's boudoir with a job lot of gold leaf and damask; and then the retro parlour with a few framed fifties pin-ups. Mo had tried something different. Tropical. An InvestNI start-up loan and a bit of money she'd saved bought her a tiny shop unit and some second-hand equipment from a liquidation auction. On the two-week start-up course they'd said about how you'd to achieve a total concept with it all working together to create brand synergy—the waiting area, the music, the décor. She had got a mate to do the painting. She had in mind a Caribbean paradise but when he'd finished it looked like a coffee shop off the Damrak. Would you like a quarter with your eyelash tint? Today's double-sell! The lights on dim and it didn't look so bad. The total concept got abandoned. The bowls of sand and shells in the waiting area should have been a good idea but people were always sticking their hands in and making the magazines gritty. After three days of *Classic Reggae: The Soundtrack to Jamaica* on repeat Mo retreated to the usual gentle ambient sounds and filled the bowls with boiled sweets.

What they said on the course didn't matter anyway because it was all about the quality of the treatments. Treatments were reasonably priced—allowing for a careful margin—and methodically executed. Nails, waxing, facials, bit of massage, fake tan. One treatment room. Total reliability: no day-release wee dolls messing things up. She was in the place for 8, ready to start at 9 and she was there for the rest of the day, six days a week. Mo was starting to get regular clients, which was good. When she opened she'd put an advert in the local free paper with a discount voucher (15%: enough to create a positive vibe) and that had got things started well. She wasn't fully booked at this stage—there were gaps in the diary—but she had known that this was how it would be for at least the first six months.

This morning Mo arrived at the same time as usual. The butcher next door was putting out his sign, a wooden cut-out cow, as Mo put up her metal shutter. Then she went through her routine: kettle on first, switch on the wax pot, light a few of the scented candles (black coconut). You needed to take away the smell of the bleach that lingered from the night before when the whole place had been washed down because ammonia wasn't very ambient. Switch on the heat: important this, although it was expensive. The place always needed to be warm because people felt awkward enough stripping down to paper pants for a tan and they didn't need to be freezing as well. The electric heater made a racket but no one had ever complained. Listen to the answer machine, turn the sign to open and finally, finally make the cup of tea.

Mo was reaching for the milk when there was a shatter of glass. She came through from the back and saw a hole in the window, a circle about two inches wide, and coming from it silver spokes that were tinkling as they crept further towards the edges of the window. Beside the table with the celeb magazines, a shiny red snooker ball had just come to rest. Mo heard the cracking of the glass, stared down at the ball, then looked at the window. Through the hole the road looked darker. She put the ball on the counter and went next door to the butcher's.

Did you hear that? Mo said. My window's just been put in.

The butcher shook his head, continued moving some meat from one tray to another. Shit, he said. That's not good. Do you need a number? For a glass place?

Yes, I do, said Mo. I can't believe that just happened.

Desperate like, he said.

I can't believe that just happened!

A woman came into the shop and he turned his attention away from Mo, did the what can I get for you my darlin?

Waiting at the bus stop outside the salon were a handful of people.

Did you see what happened there? Mo asked them. My window's just been put in.

An old fella shrugged. A boy in school uniform didn't take out his headphones.

Yeah, a man said. Car pulled up and the window went down and they threw something. Drove off quick. Did anybody get hit?

Nobody got hit, said Mo. It was just the window that got wrecked.

Bad state of affairs, said the man. Nuts.

Mo's first client of the day, in for an eyebrow wax and an eyelash tint, never commented on the window.

Blue black? Mo asked.

Blue black, the woman said.

She had taken her shoes off to lie on the bed and they sat neat in the corner, sad little comfortable shoes. Mo mixed the dye in the glass vial then smeared the Vaseline over her eyelids and under her eyes, positioned the semi-circles of paper under her bottom lashes. That window. Unfair so it was. The woman's eyelids fluttered as the dye went on, cold and wet.

That's us, said Mo. I'm going to leave you for ten minutes to let that take. You warm enough? Mo pressed two cotton wool pads on her eyes.

Oh yes, said the woman, lovely.

Good then, said Mo, and she closed the door on the woman lying blind in the dark.

The man from the glass place said he couldn't come out until tomorrow but Mo supposed that was probably as good as she was going to get; she knew that even with the insurance this was going to work out expensive, one way or another. It wasn't a total surprise it happened, she had been expecting something or other. And shouldn't she be thankful that it wasn't something worse, good that it had happened when there weren't any clients around. That fella would call in soon again, she knew it.

Mo went back into the room.

All okay?

Yes, just nodded off, said the woman. Can I stay here the rest of the day?

Mo laughed as she cleaned off the dye, firmly and precisely, and then she handed the woman a mirror to look at the transformation. Before: eyes like a rabbit's, pink and fair. After: it's all the blue black. The woman made her mirror face, an ingénue smile even though she hadn't seen sixty in years.

Oh now that's great. That's great.

The eyebrow wax took seconds, a few swift strokes. Mo mentally calculated her pay per second.

As the woman went out, the butcher came in. Here you might be needing this, he said. We had a bit left over. And he held out a length of glass repair film.

He put it on with only a couple of bubbles rising.

Kids, huh? the butcher said.

Kids, said Mo. That's good of you, I appreciate it. That's great.

Just pay it, he said. Ain't really that much, just pay it.

She hadn't spoken to him before beyond hello. She didn't talk much during the day. Alright, if it was nails, you're facing the person and it's ignorant not to, so you have to talk, but people want to keep it light, holidays and work-dos and new shops that have opened in the town. Other treatments, people just need you to shut the fuck up so let them head off to wherever they want as the cotton wool sweeps over them or your hands smooth their skin with cream. Oh there were questions you could ask if you wanted to, bodies that begged for someone to ask why, what's all that about. That long thin scar, running along the inside of your thigh, lady in the grey cashmere, what caused that? Those arms like a box of After Eights, slit slit slit, why you doing that, you with your lovely crooked smile, why you doing that? The woman with the bruises round her neck, her hand fluttering to conceal them. Jeez missus, is your fella strangling you? But you don't ask, why would you?

Mo had done enough talking, done enough listening. The call-centre job she had done at night while getting the beauty qualification had a boss called Eamonn, a man from Donegal in a velvet jacket. The pay was very poor, he had told her, below the minimum wage, but for every thirty seconds over ten minutes you kept people on the phone you got a bonus. Plus you could work all the hours you wanted pretty much, right into the night. Theresa over there, he pointed at a woman drinking tea from a flask, Theresa earns more than I do. There was a choice: either the sex line or the fortune line. Irish angle on both: guys getting off talking to colleens or women having their future decided by Celtic mystics. The other new girl said, what's with the Irish stuff? I'm not telling some fella I'm Irish when I'm not. You'll just be on the phone, the man from Donegal had said. It'll just be the accent. Which for most people, regardless of your own local distinctions, is Irish. But I'm British, she said. I'm from the loyalist community. Eamonn had looked thoughtful. No, he said. No. That's just too niche. Loyalist psychic readings. Loyalist girls wanting to talk to you now. No, my sweetheart, you are Irish to your fingertips and if you don't like it then that, and he pointed, is the door. She had stayed though and so had Mo. And what would you say, asked Mo, if you were speaking to the fellas? 'Work away there', 'keep working away there' and 'that you finished?' I'm sure you can manage something better, Mo, he had said, if you want to earn any money. Mo was put on the fortune telling. No knowledge of anything spiritual required, said Eamonn. Just keep it sensible and lengthy. If anyone is in severe straits give them the number of the Samaritans. But only after a while.

You could feel them sometimes, people's hopes, even

though all you wanted to do was just get on with your job. People looking at their faces, seeing a crumpled version staring back at them, hoping that the dermabrasion was going to make them feel like the time when they were thirty and they told that funny story at their sister's party in that restaurant and everybody laughed. For all this stuff you had to work neatly and quickly: people got nervous if you were hesitant or unsure.

Mo rolled the snooker ball in her hand. Not good. She imagined sitting down in the police station, those concerned faces when she explained what was happening, the offer to make her a cup of tea, the feigned surprise, the commitment that they would do something about it, then nothing, maybe the worse than nothing. Just pay it, the butcher had said. Ain't really that much. Well it really wasn't that much: you could recoup it with a late-night opening. But but but… that would be just the start of it. You could just see the sorry little tale taking shape: next thing it's a friend of mine's daughter needs a job, lovely girl, very keen, all those qualifications in beauty and you don't need anybody but you have to take her, and then the next thing is she arrives, hard piece, lazy-assed piece, and you are stuck with her loafing about and all her friends coming in for mates' rates. The guys next door were paying the money though and Christ knows who else on the road.

Maybe it wasn't any different to insurance. That's what the fella was implying. When he had come in before he had introduced himself and he had shaken her hand. Kyle, he said his name was. There was something about him that let her know that he was not some bloke coming in for a voucher for his missus, the only reason men came to Mo's place. She wasn't doing male treatments, no thank you, she was not doing back, sack and crack, not when she was working by herself, no way. The way he stood there, cock of the walk, like he owned the place.

With this situation there was no a, b and c. It was difficult to know what to do. That was what was wrong with the phone line, idiots wanting advice from spirits or the runes or the stars and yet it was obvious what option they should take. Kick him out! Get out of the flat! Go to a gym! Go to the doctor! Tell her the truth! Give in your notice and look for another job! Can you not understand?

One woman had phoned up about her new dream fella who just didn't get on with her ten-year-old son, had hit him quite hard one time, although fair's fair, the son had been bad, beyond cheeky. Her fella had said that the son was gonna be a problem big-time before too long and she was just so worried about the situation and wondered if she should put the son into temporary foster care, you know just temporary. Couldn't go back to being on her own again.

Pretty obvious what you should do love, isn't it?

What? the woman had said.

I said if you aren't thick as shit it is pretty obvious what you need to do, huh?

Silence on the end of the line.

People like you don't deserve to have kids. You hear that? The stars are saying that, and all the spirits in the spirit world, I can hear them coming through very clearly and they're saying you're a fuckin tool.

Mo didn't need the job any more anyway. She'd got the beauty qualification and the money saved and she was all set: a, b and c.

The next client was a full-body spray tan. Mo showed

her into the cubicle where she had laid out the paper pants. White—if it was Marilyn-white, dense and creamy—was beautiful. But people weren't ever Marilyn-white, they were lumpy and mottled. Tan helped but everyone wanted it too brown; never mind the different calibrations Mo offered, they always went for the top intensity. Mo liked doing the spray tan. You needed skill. It wasn't just point and go.

What happened your window? the woman asked, shivering a little as the tan spray moved across her tits.

Mo shrugged, concentrating on progressing to the woman's shoulder blades. Not entirely sure, she said. Young ones messing. It'll be sorted tomorrow. Hopefully anyway.

Terrible, the woman said. A place was burgled the other week.

The man, Kyle, held the door open for the woman on the way out. It gave Mo a shock to see him standing there. He wore a leather suit jacket and held a briefcase that could have come from a game show, the prize bundles inside. He put the briefcase on the table and rested on the counter.

Problem? he asked, nodding towards the window.

It'll be fixed by tomorrow, said Mo, and she started fussing at one of the shelves, aligning moisturisers.

Kyle sighed slowly, shook his head. Not good, he said. This road isn't what it used to be.

Yeah, said Mo.

The other week, he said, I was only trying to help. Seriously. This situation is just what you are trying to avoid.

Through the broken glass and the cellophane Mo could just about see a man outside, leaning against a car. She said nothing but put her hands by her sides because shit they were shaking.

You live round here? he asked.

No, said Mo. Well, not that near, she said.

Yeah, you do, said Kyle. House with the white door, number 32. Is there any point in being stupid? he said.

Mo thought of her white door.

He spread himself out in one of the seats. You see, it's like this, he began. It's all about community. Communities don't run themselves. Businesses like yours, they're vulnerable, you see what I mean? There's a lot of people out there who are not nice people and all we are really doing here, you know, if I'm being honest, is offering you our help. As a member of the community.

I know what community means, said Mo.

You do? said Kyle.

I know exactly what community means, said Mo.

On the shelf by the window there was a line of OPI nail varnishes, running the range of colours of the spectrum, twenty of them. Mo watched as he used the back of his little finger to push from the left so that the varnishes fell slowly on to the tiles, one at a time. All twenty bottles, one at a time.

Only two actually smashed, a coral and a hot red.

You need to watch it, he said.

Mo swallowed. That leather jacket would be wipe-clean.

It'll need to be in an envelope, Kyle said. And it'll be a Friday.

On his way out he turned around. And you'll also be giving me a Christmas and Easter extra. Plus something over the holiday.

I'm talking money, he said. Fuck sake don't flatter yourself love.

Hey, she shouted after him, when she knew he couldn't hear. Hey, big man! You left your ball!

Another late night it would have to be then. Nothing else for it. In the appointments book she ruled the line for Tuesday down to the bottom of the page.

~

## Kyle

The cemetery sloped down the side of the hill. Although it was big, there was rarely anyone there during the week and it was always cold up there, looking over the city. The older graves had granite surrounds and marble chips, some kept white with squirts of bleach, but most were green and mildewed. Kyle was at the lower section, the newer space, where the graves were less grandiose—just headstones side by side. He was nervous walking towards it. Over the past year there'd been the time when it had been spray painted with red loops—you wouldn't have known what it said, if it said anything—and then there was the day when someone must have taken a sledgehammer to it. They'd knocked off a great lump. Scum, pure and simple. The worst time, and Jesus this was the worst time, was when somebody had shat on the side of the tombstone. They'd smeared it across his name, David Ian Starrs, and when Kyle saw it he was disgusted to the pit of his stomach. He had only been wearing a T-shirt and he took it off, run it under the tap at the bottom of the graveyard. He attacked the stone with a fury and thought about the sound of cracking bone and the way a lip swells.

T-shirt had been stinking. He couldn't see a bin so he just bunched it up and threw it a couple of rows away where it landed on an urn.

There's a fella's feeling the heat, said a fat man who was getting a bunch of flowers out of the back seat of his car.

What did you say? Kyle went over to him. What did you just say?

Nothing mate. The man held out his hands and shook his head. No offence. It was just, you know—and he pointed at Kyle's bare chest—feeling the heat.

Kyle grabbed the bunch of dog daisies and shoved them into the man's face, right into his mouth. He was making a choking sound and the flowers were falling apart but he still kept pushing.

Who the fuck do you think you are? Kyle said, genuinely inquisitive. Like who?

He didn't tell Grace about the man and the flowers but he told her what had happened to the grave this time.

Who's responsible for doing that? she had asked.

Don't know, he said, but he knew it could be several different people, several different groups. Davy's funeral had actually been on the TV, well the local news at six in the evening, but by the later news something else had replaced it. Afterwards they had sat in the bar with Davy's three little children marauding around and the two practically identical ex-partners. But today the grave was fine and nobody had touched it. Kyle traced the golden lettering with his finger.

Grace had said that they were going out for their dinner that night but he had not been enthusiastic. Well, we're going, she had said, and that's that.

Why? he had asked.

Just are. It's bring your own, so if you want to, bring your own. It's just new opened. I met the guy who runs it's wife.

Do we have to?

Yes.

Well, I got stuff to do. Tell me where it is and I'll just meet you there.

Kyle's stuff. A diverse portfolio. He had heard somebody say that once and he had liked it so he used it. Things had been better though: money came in well enough most of the time, but it wasn't always easy to maintain control. The taxi company, such as it was, did all right delivering the after-hours what have you, and then there was the shop and the mechanics that he had a main cut in. Most places were still paying up, as were the small dealers, but nothing felt secure. What was it? It was just—maybe it wasn't any different from what it had ever been and it was just him. Davy going had been terrible. That coroner: heart attack brought on by steroid abuse, no way was Kyle having that. Why wasn't everybody having heart attacks then if that was the case? Basically the enemy was everywhere and there wasn't anybody left to trust except Grace who he did trust even though she probably disapproved of everything. Once, when there was a situation, she had been taken in for questioning for a day and a half and she had said nothing. In fact, one of them had said to him, you're punching above with that one Kyle. There were Hungarians on the scene now, they smashed up one of the bars and they were making inroads into things. And your woman, lippy fuck, going on about community the other day, oh I know about community, should've firebombed the place. Might still. The sort of people that were coming up now, they weren't the same. Boys were stupid, the ones who would have been part of it in the past now went to university, cleared out.

But maybe it was just him. That was why he was going to try this place, against his better judgment. A flyer had come through the door about it but it was far enough away for very few people to recognise him. It was above a dry cleaners. He'd been past the other day to see what it looked like, the Class A Hypnotherapy. Just a staircase up and then some net curtains. Looked a dump, but if it worked it worked. Nothing else—and he had tried a lot of stuff—had made any difference.

The waiting room was a small white cube and on the wall there were testimonials from people who had been successfully treated at Class A Hypnotherapy. There was some ponce who he had never heard of saying that Class A had cured him of his stage fright and that he was ready to do a summer season in Blackpool for the first time in years. Fella looked a fruit, him and his nerves. Fuck him and his nerves. And then there was some student who had written to say that her troubles had cleared up thanks to yeah yeah yeah. There was a candle oil burner and the place smelled of a plant and the music was like you'd get in a Chinese. Kyle lifted out the candle and burned along the edge of one of the brochures on the table, setting fire to an inch or so at a time, and then blowing it out. When he'd done around the whole brochure he blew out the candle.

He heard voices, somebody coming out of the room and going down the stairs, and then a man appeared in the waiting room. Geoff, he said, extending his hand. Very pleased to meet you.

Kyle stood up.

And you are, he got a diary out of his pocket, you are—

Marty, said Kyle.

Well, Marty, please come on through.

The Chinese music was still on the go in the other room and there was a beige sofa where Kyle was told to sit because there needed to be a consultation before any treatment could begin.

We need to fill in a questionnaire, said Geoff. Your other name, Marty?

Kyle thought for a minute. The only thing that came to mind was Pellow.

Pellow, he said.

Alright, said Geoff, as he filled the boxes. Marty Pellow. Address?

Look no, said Kyle. Never mind my address. Are you gonna just get on with this?

I do need your GP's name, said Geoff with an apologetic smile. Who would your GP be now, Marty?

Arches, he said.

Right you are, said Geoff, writing in The Arches Medical Centre. So, he said, admin done, what brings you along to us today?

Kyle shrugged. Just the usual.

Geoff continued to look at him, his pen poised. Just what, Marty? How do you feel?

Alright.

You feel alright. What would alright be on a scale of 1 to 10?

Jeez. Seven out of ten, Kyle said. Maybe an eight.

Now that, said Geoff, is really quite good.

Yeah, so? said Kyle.

If most days you feel seven, maybe an eight, then why, Marty, have you come to see us?

There's only you here, yeah? asked Kyle. Why you keep saying us? Why you keep saying that when it's only you?

People come to us for all sorts of reasons, Geoff continued. Some want to give up smoking say, others have a specific fear, of flying perhaps, or maybe they feel nervous thinking about a particular event.

Kyle's face showed his opinion of these kinds of people.

And then there are those who come to us because they experience high levels of anxiety, manifest quite possibly in panic attacks, sleeplessness, or obsessive-compulsive disorders—

Alright, said Kyle, don't be telling me any more about these people, I don't care. Could we just get on with whatever it is you do like, you know, maybe now. If that's convenient.

Geoff indicated a chair over in the corner. You sure you want to continue, Marty? he said. There's not a lot of point in continuing if you feel this isn't for you. The will must be there.

Well, he wasn't expecting it to be a man swinging a watch on a chain and saying look into my eyes but this was just a chair with your man perched on the desk, but then the chair reclined, like a La-Z-Boy, but so far back it wasn't a telly you were watching, it was the ceiling. There was a black spot on the ceiling. The man had gone out and come back with a blanket and a cushion that had been heated up.

Kyle threw the cushion on the floor. I don't think we'll be needing that, mate. He kicked off the blanket. All this shit would you just make a start here?

Geoff started to say the spiel. He was reading it off, you could tell, the way he was savouring every word. Something about a beach and the sun shining: yeah, he could imagine the beach, he could imagine a few hot birds in bikinis, okay well now they were starting to get off with each other. Well, that was pretty all right to think about, but Geoff said *Focus* really loud and then he was back to the room, listening to that voice of his going on about different parts of the body. That Chinese music was still on the go, the ribs and the black bean sauce, wee doll bringing over a sizzling dish, you spinning that revolving table. Mandarin City. Cueball ate the fortune cookie at the end, bit of paper and all. How the fuck was I meant to know, he said, give me yours and I'll eat it as well. That was a while ago though, some laugh, that fella was long gone.

Geoff was saying to think about contentment, when you felt in control, and Kyle is in the old front room where their dad is lying half on, half off the rug and the blood from his mouth is pooling on the floor. A couple of weeks before Davy had asked, you know the way I'm fourteen and you know the way you're thirteen? You put us together do we equal a man of twenty-seven? Must have put it into their heads they could swing it—and they did because when the old fella hit Davy full on the face the two of them laid into him and there he was on the floor. Still dangerous because they couldn't afford for him to get either one of them alone, but even that would only be for a certain period of time because they were getting stronger and his boozing was getting worse. Pathetic him lying there. Felt good to see the legs collapse from under him, pathetic the way he tried to appeal to them through the blood. Davy! And then, Kyle!

Even their ma was pleased. She said oh what's the world coming to, and all of that stuff, but she was happy and they knew it. She put a tea towel over his head. And that was what Kyle was thinking of, that was a good day.

Try to take a snapshot of that contentment, focus on a detail of that scene if you can, said Geoff, are you focusing Marty, on something specific? (Yes: the blood on the floor way darker than you'd think.) Can you do that, Marty? That's good. Good. You are going to hold that in your mind as a motif of happiness that you can refer to. You holding it in your mind?

I am, said Kyle.

And how are you feeling? asked Geoff.

Okay.

You're feeling good? asked Geoff.

Okay, said Kyle.

Hold that image and know that you are the same person who can achieve that contentment again, whenever you want, Marty.

But no, Kyle thought. No. Because Davy wasn't here and that made everything not the same. What the fuck was he doing lying with a blanket round him on a chair above the dry cleaners listening to this pure shite, how bad had things got that this was what he was at?

Right, that's it. Over, that's enough. Will you move this fucking—he tried to push himself out of the chair—this fucking—

Geoff spoke calmly. The initial session can sometimes be a little underwhelming. Next time—

There'll be no next time, said Kyle. That's it.

Geoff took an invoice from a pad at the desk, calmly filled it in, and handed it to Kyle.

You got to be having a laugh, he said. Eighty quid to lie back in a chair and listen to you reading a script off a page, well I do not think so. Here, he hoked around in the pocket of his jacket, that'll do you, and he handed him a fiver. You are making easy money, pal, let me tell you with this fucking caper.

Geoff watched from the window as Kyle got into his car, slammed the door shut.

Kyle Starrs, he said aloud.

The restaurant had had a refit since it had been the burger bar. There were now white tiles and pictures from local artists. Every table had a couple of tea lights and a posy in a jam jar. Grace was already there, sitting at the table. Kyle came in, clinking with bottles.

Can I take those for you? the fella asked.

Kyle lifted out two bottles of Moët, and a bottle of Courvoisier.

One of those over in an ice bucket, he said. What? he said to Grace.

Nothing.

It's bring your own, yeah?

It's bring your own.

Well, then. What's the issue?

She sighed. Doesn't matter.

It's bring your own and I've brought my own. Jesus Christ.

The young man brought over the menus.

I'm actually quite hungry, Grace said. Haven't eaten anything all day.

Well, order whatever you want. Here, what's the hold-up with the drink? Kyle said. Oi! Mate! He pointed to the table. Drink?

The fella came over, apologetic. It's just that, we don't

have any ice buckets yet. We're only open, I mean, we're only just open so not everything's quite right yet.

Grace smiled at him. No problem, she said.

Hick joint, said Kyle when the waiter had gone. Don't think much of this place.

Wise up, Kyle, Grace said. Just leave it for goodness sake.

The fella came back with the champagne, glasses and an improvised ice bucket in the form of a vase. Oh, not for me, Grace said when, having filled Kyle's, the waiter went to pour her a glass. I'm happy with this. She pointed to her tonic water.

Right you are, he said.

When the fella moved to the next table, Kyle poured Grace a glass of champagne. Cheers, he said.

I don't want any, Kyle. I said to you.

God, a glass won't kill you.

I don't want it.

There was no enjoyment in drinking by yourself. That voice of hers killed him. Always calm. He once had said to her, you know who you remind me of? Clint Eastwood.

That's flattering, she said.

I know it is, he had replied.

But she could make you feel like nothing. She wasn't impressed by much: a five star would mean as much as a two star. Jewellery she wasn't into. Not interested in fancy places, well that was obvious when you took a look around here. They could have been in the town at somewhere where you got treated really well, where there were plenty of people about to see you out and about. He knew fine rightly that she knew about the various other women over the years, but she never made a scene. He wouldn't have minded her being bothered, full-on furious, he wouldn't have minded if she'd punched and slapped him. Even that one time when your woman that he had seen on and off for a few months came around to the house to make a row, she had just said, a friend of yours to see you, and gone out of the house. Did your woman ever regret that one, but Grace never mentioned it again other than to say, please try to avoid that kind of thing, Kyle, because I could do without it.

The young fella was over asking them if they had decided what they wanted. Grace said she would have the pulled pork and Kyle said he wanted the steak. He hadn't looked at the menu, but he wanted the steak.

Well done, he said. I like it, you know, really well done.

The fella went away and then came back. It's just, he said, it's just that the chef says that it's a minute steak.

So what? Kyle said.

Minute steaks are meant to be cooked quickly. That's what the chef says, he added carefully.

No, said Kyle. Well cooked. End of.

Grace leaned across the table. They're only saying that if you want it well done, it's likely to be tough because minute steaks need to be fried quick.

Did we come out for a cookery lesson? Did we? Minute steak. What a load of shite.

The woman appeared at the table. We're sorry about the steak situation, she said. Maybe there's something else on the menu that you would like to choose.

No love, said Kyle. I've made my order, thank you very much.

Were you busy today? Grace asked.

Kyle shrugged. Just the usual. Was up at the grave, he said.

Used to be small, that graveyard, said Grace. It's eaten

up most of that hill now. Everybody all together in that graveyard, she said.

Yeah well, said Kyle. Death comes to us all. Grim Reaper.

Does that steak come with sauce? Can't remember, he said. I don't want the sauce all over the top of it. I hate when they do that, slather the sauce all over the top of it.

The young fella came over to top up Kyle's glass of champagne.

You celebrating something? he asked.

No, said Kyle. That guy's doing my head in, he said to Grace when he had gone.

He's just doing his job Kyle, she said.

The steak, when it arrived, was a pathetic specimen, a shrivelled offering.

Well you got what you asked for, said Grace. You can't complain. So don't complain.

Kyle tried to cut it but it didn't yield.

Fucking shoe leather, he said. That's gonna bounce off the walls.

Try some of this, said Grace. It's nice. We'll share it and they can bring us another plate.

So I've come out for half a meal, he thought. I can't even get a proper meal. That ponce, what had he said to think about, what did he tell me, and he thought, yes, it was his da lying half on half off the rug. Davy had wanted to wrap that electric flex around his neck, the one that he used to hit them, but he had said no just leave it, that was enough, enough for now. Sore being hit with that flex.

~

## Grace

The worst was the street-preaching when they stood in Cornmarket on a Saturday afternoon with two speakers, a microphone and a cardboard box full of tracts. If it rained they put the box in a black bin bag. On the rare occasion they went to places like Portadown or Lurgan and Grace didn't mind this so much because there would be no chance of seeing anyone from school. It would be the usual: you'd be cold and you'd get people either shouting abuse or laughing at you, but at least no one would know who you were.

There were things you could do to pass the time. You could count the paving stones for as far as they stretched into the distance; they started square and then, as they got further and further away, became wafers. You could hold your breath until you saw someone with a pink coat. Then you could hold your breath until you saw someone with a green coat. Then you could hold your breath until you saw someone in brown boots. You could do those same things in Cornmarket but you had no anonymity. Three o'clock on a Saturday afternoon there would be all the shrieking laughing crowd from school. Is that not your wee woman from our year? Your wee doll in that big coat? It is her. Feel wick for her. Shout something over but.

Sometimes there would be competition from other groups: fire-eaters, choirs and, now and again, breakdancers who would bring a CD player and turn it up loud until the sound broke. Grace's dad would turn up the preacher's volume and his sound won out because it had an amp. It was a cosmic battle between good and evil right there in

Cornmarket, transmogrified into a street sermon versus 2 Unlimited.

An American evangelist had held an old-time crusade in a huge white tent on the O'Neill Road and the very first night he went Grace's dad had some kind of epiphany. On the next evening Grace's mum had one too. They started going to a mission hall that was opposite an old dairy and constructed out of corrugated iron. Women had to wear hats. There were some people who had apparently been very bad like Jimmy Baker who had given his testimony and told everyone about how he had found the Lord after being a gambler and a womaniser and a communist street fighter. Jimmy Baker seemed so nice, sucking his mints in the back row.

Sunday clothes were uncomfortable in ways you could not have imagined. The tights were always too small and the good wool skirt scratched. The label on the nape of the jacket was stiff but it was stitched right in so you couldn't cut it out. The hat was like a pancake. There were lots of ways you could wear a beret, Grace's mother had said. Yeah and every one of them stupid. The shop windows showed bright clothes, tight clothes. You walked past people, women, and they were all like the drawings in the maths book with the compass, soft concurrent semicircles. Grace's clothes, bought at charity shops, were chosen for their amorphous quality. Her mother talked about 'good' materials, wools, gabardine, camel hair, durable and decent. The girls in her class used tampons. Grace's mother thought tampons tantamount to rape.

The preacher was called the Reverend Dr Emery. Everything he said was in groups of three. Sin, despair and iniquity. Our Saviour past present and future. A strong, hot, welcome cup of tea, available at the back of the church after the service. The long, boring, repetitive service. You could stare at the Reverend Dr Emery in the pulpit until he doubled and became surrounded in black light and then you could look at the ceiling and see his outline in relief against the whitewashed beams. You could make bargains with the Lord. I will believe if you make your woman there's hat fall off. She scratches her neck. Split second when you think it might happen. Hat stays on. You could listen to tales from a mostly Old Testament world of hard justice. You could listen to his lamenting tone: oh why is the world filled with such evil? You could think: I don't know if I believe this.

Then the Carson family started coming. They were tall, thin people, a husband and wife, who had been in Malawi for many years, mostly working on bible translation but involved in other projects too. Their own children had long left home but they fostered kids, short term, and they had plenty of room in their big double-fronted house with the overgrown garden. First there was a boy, about ten, who had a hearing aid and a green coat. Grace wondered if he could hear what the Reverend Dr Emery said; he mouthed the hymns like he was dubbed. Then there was an older boy, although he wasn't there for that long, whose head was always cocked to one side; oh aye right, it said. Then there was a girl who overlapped with him for a month or so, fat with a pale face. Grace's mother had said, why don't you go over and talk to her after church, so Grace had tried but the girl hadn't asked her anything back. Grace shifted from foot to foot until it was time to go. And then there was the next one who had a clump of hair dyed pink. After one of the bible readings she shouted out, Amen! and then started laughing. There was embarrassed, irritated shooshing. Later, Grace's mum said, I think that girl's a bit lacking. Shouting out like that. People don't shout out like that in our church.

She did it with an American accent, said Grace.

She's a bit lacking.

But that didn't stop Grace's mother asking her to go around to help the girl, Kerri, with her schoolwork.

Why? said Grace. It didn't go well, speaking to the other one.

This is a different girl. She needs help with her schoolwork.

Why can't Mrs Carson help her?

She's busy. You're going round tonight. I said to them that you would.

Like I'm the genius.

Don't be cheeky, Grace, her mother had said.

Mrs Carson said the bedroom was the first door on the right at the top of the stairs. Should she knock? Grace wasn't sure.

Hello, she called.

What you want? the girl Kerri said from inside. And then she came to the door. What you want?

I'm meant to help you with stuff, said Grace. That's what they said for me to come and do.

Who?

Them.

What stuff?

School stuff.

I don't go to school, Kerri said.

Then why did they send me?

I go to a centre.

They said I was to help you.

Well, I don't want any help, Kerri said and closed the door.

But her mother sent her back again the next night. Sometimes it's necessary to persevere. We need to do what we can where we can.

Not you again, Kerri said, opening her door when Grace knocked. Behind her everything was around the bed like a magnet: clothes, magazines, dirty tights with the knickers still in them, cans of coke. You could smell body spray but mainly smoke. Did the Carsons not notice?

Did you not get the message last time? she said. Why you here again?

Mrs Carson called them downstairs. Kerri screwed up her face. On the dining-room table there was a book with a rabbit on the front cover and a worksheet. The other kids were playing out in the garden, even though it was raining a bit. Mrs Carson said, Kerri, I want you to remember the talk we had earlier. You remember? No effort made with work, no allowance. No allowance, no whatever it is you like to buy.

Kerri scowled across the table at Grace. Then she lifted the book about the rabbit and opened it at a random page. Her finger slowly ran under each word and her lips silently formed the words. She read about ten pages like this, with Grace looking on redundant.

Then she sighed, closed the book. Done, she said.

What's it about? asked Grace.

Fucking rabbit, said Kerri. Did you not see the front of it?

Is that what you have to read?

If it wasn't, you think I'd be looking at it huh?

It's a rabbit that goes around doing stuff, she added.

She dropped the book on the floor.

The other one was about a homeless man, she said.

Was it better? Grace asked.

No, said Kerri.

Come on up the stairs, she said. I want to show you something.

Grace thought that Mrs Carson might object but she was involved in doing something in the kitchen and so said nothing. Grace found herself sitting on Kerri's rumpled bed. Kerri was pulling something out from behind her wardrobe. She sat down on the bed beside Grace with a magazine.

Never mind that, look at this, she said.

She opened the magazine at a page where there was a woman lying on a sofa with her legs wide open. Not totally naked: she had on gold platform heels.

What do you think of that then? said Kerri, holding it up close to Grace's face.

Grace said nothing.

What do you think of that?

She turned to another page with two women.

And that?

Never you mind you coming round here to tell me about this that or yon, you don't know it all. Look at it again. Look at this one. They're all at it. All that lot in that tin box just the same as everyone else.

You're not normal, Kerri went on. You're really weird. I seen you sitting there with those two, your mum and dad, all holy holy, and I think, God help you. You know Helen Watson who used to live here, well she said the same thing about you. Said you were a psycho.

You're the one who's not normal, said Grace.

Oh aye is that right? I'm not going round like a granny mush fucking mouse. What you frightened of? Burning in hell?

No, said Grace. I'm not going to burn in hell.

Here let me tell you something, said Kerri. Let me tell you something. What year were you born in? What year was it?

1980, said Grace.

1980. So in 1979 you weren't here. Were you bothered? You weren't. So when you're not here again because you're dead, will you be bothered? No. You weren't before—so you won't be again.

Grace thought about this.

Hah! said Kerri. Think about that one. Put that in your pipe and smoke it. Aw, but no, you can't because Jesus says don't smoke.

1979. It was a nothing.

Kerri started reading the description of the woman from the magazine. Here listen, she said. Listen to this. She read it with a big pause between each word, the cadence of a kid, following the line with her finger. Cindy... likes... Cindy likes—

What? said Grace. What is it Cindy likes?

Kerri puzzled at the word.

Maybe, said Grace, maybe you should stick to the rabbit book, Kerri.

Kerri rolled up the mag and threw it at Grace. Read it yourself, she said.

Grace grabbed it, twisted it tight and hit Kerri across the cheek with it.

I didn't want to come here. Do you understand that?

Kerri came charging across the room, grabbed Grace by

the hair and threw her onto the bed, elbowed her hard in the gut. Grace gasped—she couldn't breathe out. But it was easier to hit Kerri than she would have thought; her fist made contact with her stomach, taut as a drum, and she hit her again and again. They fell onto the floor on top of the dirty tights and the dirty plates. Kerri was quick and heavy, the ways she flipped Grace over, twisting her arm up behind her back. She couldn't move and Kerri kept pushing harder so that she thought she was going to be sick. And then Kerri stopped. She was panting, trying to catch her breath. All Grace could smell was fags and hot fabric conditioner. Mrs Carson must put loads in the washes. Kerri took another handful of her hair and Grace thought she was going to get hit again but instead Kerri's mouth was soft although you could taste the blood like a coin.

At home Grace's mother was sewing a hem.

All go well? she asked.

It was alright, Grace said.

There are some booklets you could take round next time. There's those new ones that were sent from the States.

Sure, said Grace.

Her mother's hand stretched the thread taut, did a final double stitch and cut the thread.

When they were next in church there was a big empty space at the end of the pew where the Carsons sat. Kerri wasn't there. It was the same the week after and the week after that. After church Mrs Carson said that she was grateful that Grace had helped Kerri along a bit, but that she had gone back to live with her mother now. They come and they go, Mrs Carson said. This is for you, she said. She gave Grace a folded up piece of paper with an address and phone number on it. The frill of a spiral bound page torn off. Big bubble writing: written with careful deliberation, nearly pressed through the page. She kept the paper even though she knew that she was never going to phone or call round. She couldn't imagine it: going to the pictures with Kerri; going for a meal with Kerri. Sending each other a Valentine: it seemed preposterous.

The next week Grace didn't go to church. She said it was because she wasn't well, but when her mother came up to her room, she said the thing is I'm giving going to church a miss for the time being. She knew that they prayed for her all the time. They sent Reverend Dr Emery around to see her and she sipped a cup of tea slowly while he told her about lost sheep and the prodigal son. He tried to scare her by talking about girls he had heard of who had strayed from the righteous path and who, without exception, had come to a bad end. They would congregate at the front door, there would be whispering and then he would go. There would invariably be a quiet knock on her door. Everything alright, Grace? Her mother would be hopeful. Fine, Grace would nod.

There was pain and there was passion and there was no God. Some people had to wait a lifetime to find out that kind of thing, had to study and read books, gaze up at the stars. But it had been made apparent to her when she was young, it had come all in a rush when someone was whacking her with a porno mag. You might never experience that intensity of revelation ever, ever again.

You lived your life. You didn't expect anything too much. There were holidays and meals and trips to the multiplex and city breaks. There was work in the nursery, which was good fun most of the time. All that intensity was a long time ago now. She loved Kyle and wouldn't leave him.

Would he have been like how he was if it hadn't been for that brother of his, getting him into stuff? Good riddance to Davy. Live by the sword die by the sword. Matthew 26: 52. She could remember that. Grace had found out she couldn't have kids. They had tried IVF but it hadn't worked. She had been frightened he would go off with one of the others but he didn't. Doesn't matter, he said. I've got you and that's what matters. Sex was useless because she felt a dud.

She went to church one time, nostalgic for her youth, when she saw a poster for a crusade, but it was a small scale affair that took place in a hall where the floor was marked out for badminton and basketball with coloured tape. All the people were old and had all been saved years ago. There was no singing, only a man and a PowerPoint, but she ended up helping out with the teas because there was something wrong with the urn.

This morning Grace was leaving stuff at the dry cleaners and then going to the beauty place. She had been there practically every other week since it opened. She had never thought before that she was high maintenance, but now it turned out that she was. She wouldn't have thought of going there if she hadn't seen the advert and the voucher in the paper. The woman was just starting out. Weird little box of a place but she liked it. It was always warm, and it smelled of coconut. The girl didn't say much which was good. The first time she had gone, it had been for a leg wax. It was sore. The woman had said, next time, take a couple of paracetamol before you come. You know what in fact, she had said, take a couple of paracetamol and a brandy. Can only make it better. She had taken neither the paracetamol nor the brandy. The girl's face was sometimes only a couple of inches away from you: you could run your finger along that frown of concentration. That ponytail, you could wrap it round and round your fist, pull it tight. She always looked preoccupied. Grace thought about her all the time. What did other people think of? Lying on beaches? Being in the Caribbean? To do lists? Grace thought about the taste of blood, a woman in gold high heels, lying face down on a bed. It was a disappointment every time when the woman said, well that's it, I'll leave you to get ready and I'll see you outside. The dull thud of the well this is all there is.

And here she was again, back for more, sitting waiting for the woman to get the room ready. She looked at the line of moisturisers, the row of nail varnishes, the stack of magazines.

What happened the window? Grace asked when the girl appeared.

It'll be fixed this morning, she said, if the fella ever arrives. Go on into the room, it's all set up, and I'll be through in a minute.

# Inakeen

Jean's son Malcolm had decided to make one of his infrequent visits. He took the seat in front of the television and when he turned it on she heard him let out his usual sigh at the poor choice of channels. Jean was positioned at the end of the sofa because it gave the best view out the window.

Malcolm was telling her that he had a new boss. The boss had only been in the job a couple of weeks but Malcolm didn't like him. Some of the others did, up to them, but he didn't.

Only a couple of weeks, Jean said. Still early days then really, isn't it?

Early days and already not going well, Malcolm said.

Across the road Jean saw the fluid bulk of Black Sail appear, wrestling along a bin bag with both hands. Then the door opened a little wider and there was Inakeen, holding what looked to be a huge candle. No, but not a candle, the base of a standard lamp in fact. Bin bag and candle went in the bin. No sign of W7. Maybe she was working. But now there she was.

Malcolm took out his phone and began scrolling through the photos.

Another thing by the way. I've a new girlfriend, he said.

Oh?

Yeah. Was going to show you a photo but I can't seem to find the one I was looking for.

His new girlfriend, he said, was based in Scotland, near Paisley, and was only in Belfast one week in every four. That suited him just fine because he wouldn't get fooled again. He repeated it for emphasis. I won't get fooled again. Both he and the new girlfriend understood that they would be operating on an easy come easy go basis.

Well, there you are then, Jean said.

So don't be getting your hopes up or anything, he said. Because it's all strictly casual.

Six months ago, when they came, Black Sail was the first one that Jean saw: Black Sail, conspicuous anonymity, sitting on the wall opposite her own. Behind was the cherry blossom and beyond that, the cream render of the house. The edge of the bedroom curtain touched Jean's cheek as she peered down. She watched as two young boys passed by, staring. After a few steps, they stopped in their tracks and turned around again to gawp but Black Sail, unperturbed, merely crossed one hand slowly over the other. Just—like—that. Impatient then, Black Sail got up and walked as far as the next house, then back again, billowing a bit in the wind, just like a black sail. So that, immediately was what she became. Black Sail had a black rucksack over one shoulder. She took her seat on the wall once more, kicking what looked like a small stone from one foot to the other. Then a car drew up and a fat man in a suit got out. The old tenants had left two weeks ago, that family with the kids who always left their colourful paraphernalia in the driveway. The man was probably from the rental place, looking to move new people in. Another car drew up. A woman, later to be known as W7 was driving and when the mother, Inakeen, got out she didn't close the door properly, didn't do it hard enough. Even from looking that was obvious. W7 had pointed to it and said something, probably that the central locking wasn't going to work unless the door was closed properly. Well, it was easy enough to be too gentle with a car door. But Black Sail had come over and given it a heavy slam before proceeding towards the others with a rolling, unhurried walk. Everyone went inside and then, ten minutes later, they came out and drove off. It wasn't a mansion so it only required a short viewing.

Jean had waited for Malcolm to ask her how she was.

To be honest, Malcolm, I haven't been up to much myself, she eventually said. There was an accident on the dual carriageway earlier on today. I heard so many sirens.

Yeah?

Yes. I wouldn't be surprised if somebody's been killed. Ambulances, police, fire engines.

Don't know, never heard anything about it.

I'm sure it's been on the news.

Don't know. Oh this. He settled on a film to watch. Seen this before. The guys in this are muppets.

I was actually in town the other night, Jean said.

Yeah?

I haven't been in town in the evening for a long time.

OK.

Yes.

There you go then, he said. Something different. Being in the town.

I was at an exhibition of photos.

Right.

I was at a competition for members of these different photography clubs. They were showing some of the entries in a place round the back of that old church. Near the lingerie shop.

A photography exhibition. Different clubs, she said. A competition.

So, Malcolm said, it was like, you'd entered it.

Yes, I'd entered.

You win anything?

No, I didn't win anything.

In fact, even though the gallery walls were hung with numerous photos, Jean's hadn't even made the cut for general display.

Better luck next time, said Malcolm. Jeez this guy's so dumb. He actually didn't even notice she had a gun.

When Jean was first on her own she was advised to join groups, the general belief being that it would prevent her descent into some kind of slough of despond. Initially she tried a book club at the library but she could rarely get beyond the first chapter, when the books had chapters. Sometime later she produced anaemic scenes in a watercolour class and felt only relief when the teacher said that the group would not continue after the summer months. Most recently she had become a member of a club which necessitated the purchase of a camera, because it was a camera club. The only other woman at the club was a divorcee called Angie. That was the first thing that she had told Jean about herself: recently divorced and all very acrimonious. Some weeks at the camera club had been theoretical so, for example, they had sat in a circle to hear about apertures. The practical sessions were themed:

one week it was musical instruments and then the next portraiture. Some of the men hadn't wanted to photograph each other and the tutor, Sam, had had to give them a prim little lecture on the importance of the objective eye. There were a couple of field trips, one to an abandoned farm where they took photographs of rust on corrugated iron and light streaming through broken roofs, and another to Carrickfergus Castle. On that occasion there was the opportunity to take photos of a young woman in a white dress.

Jean saw that the door was opening again. Ah, Inakeen, with the cup. That was how she watered the plants in the three tubs outside the house, going backwards and forwards with the cup. Did she not think about getting a watering can? Even a big saucepan would have done the job. Perhaps she was worried about deluging them. If Inakeen was only coming to the door, she didn't wear the full rigmarole so it was possible to catch a glimpse of her pinched little face. Black Sail? Only the eyes. Only ever the eyes. W7, the whole face, a toffee penny.

Malcolm won't get fooled again after the split from Mariel, the mother of his three-year-old son, Anton. On one of the days after her husband died, when people sat around the perimeter of the room, making conversation that drifted from banal to profound and back again as the tea cooled in their cups, Jean watched as hands with some kind of reminder scrawled on them lifted the tray from the coffee table in the centre. When she went out to the kitchen, Jean saw that someone had washed and put everything away. Then Malcolm appeared.

This is Mariel, he said, putting his arm around her waist. She's Canadian.

Well, you are, he said.

Thanks for reminding me, Mariel said.

She gave Jean a smile that was a wink.

Mariel was from outside Quebec City. The foreignness in her voice never quite went away even after Jean had spent hours, days with her. Malcolm's other girlfriends, the ones she had met, had had a sweaty glamour, all glowing skin and cleavage. Under Mariel's shapeless clothes there was sinew. Her lank hair was tied back with an elastic band. When Malcolm told Jean that he was to become a father she thought that either he or Mariel must have miscalculated somehow because the two of them didn't seem suited at all.

Maybe you need a better camera, Malcolm said. Nikon D Series. Meant to be really good. You heard of that?

No. Well, I've heard of Nikon. But not the D Series.

Might be the problem you know. Maybe you've just not got the right equipment.

I don't know if the camera makes much difference.

Costs about 500 quid this camera. So, probably about 400 quid difference, minimum, to what you have.

I don't know.

You get what you pay for, Malcolm said. Got to say I think that's very true.

Jean shrugged.

It would make a difference, Malcolm said. Believe me.

I'm in a wine club, he said. See between 5 quid and 20 quid? Massive jump in quality. For something really special you obviously need to go dearer. Personally I wouldn't spend less than twenty. Every couple of months all of us in the club go to some restaurant, you know, fine dining, wines in triple figures. Sommeliers—the whole shebang. That's wine guys, he added.

After the initial sighting of Black Sail, Inakeen and W7, Jean saw nothing of them for some time. She did not notice them move in; it must have happened in the dead of night. But one day a trip to the shops revealed W7 and Inakeen in the vegetable aisle, looking at the net bags of onions. Others watched them too, although they feigned interest in the shelves. Then Black Sail came into view, striding along with a twelve-pack of crisps. Inakeen! she said, her voice impatient, and she gestured over to the till. Inakeen. Jean said it to herself later on when she was sitting in her living room. She liked the gentle cadence of it. It sounded the kind of name someone would call their house but it meant mother, mum, mummy perhaps. Inakeen was obviously older, her movements more tentative.

Jean grabbed a bag of oranges and followed them to the till. She could see the girl behind one of the counters, the one with the flurry of stars tattooed down the side of her face, mentally calculating at which till the women in black were likely to end up and it looked like she didn't want it to be hers. Black Sail's rucksack had a broken zip, Inakeen's brown leather bag a buckle and a shoulder strap. W7's was decorated with tiny diamantes and embroidery. Inakeen's hand rested on the top of the bag, small and in colour not so very different to the bag itself, except the leather was smoother. The laughter behind Jean came from two teenage girls who were holding up their phones. Hey yous! one said. Hey yous! Then the girl turned to her friend. There's no way that is anything other than totally fucking weird, she said. Seriously fucked up way to go around the place like. Tick—tick—tick—boom! Jean moved slightly to look at the end aisle display, temporarily obstructing their view.

I don't suppose you've been in contact with Mariel? Jean asked Malcolm.

He sighed again.

I was just wondering.

No mother, I haven't. Not in the last couple of weeks. But I suppose you have.

Would I be right?

She had, but it had only been brief, and on the computer. Anton couldn't wait to get away to play with some toy so Mariel had to keep forcing him to sit on her knee. Mariel kept pointing at Jean, saying Mamie! Mamie! Anton stared momentarily at the old woman on the screen and then the computer froze. It worked for thirty seconds, and then froze again.

Here we go, Malcolm said. Wondered how long it would be before you brought the subject up. Wondered how long it would be before the subject would turn to that bitch. So, tell me all about it. Tell me all about Mariel and tell me all about Anton, my son.

They seemed fine, Jean said. It was only very briefly I was speaking to them.

Right, he said.

Anton's getting bigger, Jean said.

Child in growth shocker.

Malcolm, said Jean. Come on.

Never wanted to call him Anton. Never did. Anton. Sounds like a name you'd give a waiter. Do you know what I wanted? Lawrence, after Dad. But no, that wouldn't do, all Mariel, as per bloody usual, so that's why we ended up with Anton. Never liked it as a name, never wanted it.

It's just a name, Jean said, wondering if there was so very much of a difference between Anton and Lawrence.

42

Well, the whole thing's a fucking joke. I've got a son who, well, putting aside the fact that he actually lives halfway across the world, doesn't even speak the same language as me. I mean, Jesus. French. *J'habite à Belfast. Ou est le restaurant.* Christ almighty, fucking French.

Fewer people learn languages these days, Jean said. They're in decline.

Malcolm used to come home from school, dump his bag at the door, then retreat to his room to watch videos, as it was then. He'd wanted blackout curtains in the room because the other ones let in too much light when he was watching whatever it was he watched. She'd bought them for him, got a duvet cover to match.

Little wonder, he said. Waste of time. *J'habite à Belfast. Ou est le restaurant.*

Jean had gone to their house most days when Anton was just a new baby. If the weather was good she and Mariel would walk long, looping routes with the pram, up one side of the road and down the other, past charity shops, chemists, cafes, hairdressers. If it was wet, they might stay in to watch a film, whatever was on the TV, a western or a romance, it didn't really matter. The blow heater was always on. It was warm. There was the coddling noise of the steriliser, the warmth of the baby, the hot washing and milk smell.

Jean missed Mariel and Anton more than she did Lawrence. Her husband was someone she once overheard being described as a fellow who would put a bob on himself both ways. And whoever it was said to didn't care to disagree. But death was a kind release for the diminished man lying in the hospital, eyes staring at a never-ending news programme. With the departure of Mariel and Anton, however, there was no counterbalance. She could try if she wanted to think of Mariel as the bitch as Malcolm did, but she knew that she wasn't.

One day, as they took turns pushing the pram, Mariel said to Jean that there was something she had to tell her. And the thing she had to tell her was that she and Malcolm were going to split up.

Definitely? Jean asked.

Oh yes definitely, Mariel said. Absolutely.

Oh my goodness.

Does it really come as a surprise to you, Jean?

No, she said. Not really.

Jean wondered how Malcolm felt about it.

About us splitting up? Mariel shrugged. Well, he feels the same way. That's it. Over. He's going to move out next week. He's going to stay with a friend. No, not like that. Just a friend. Friend friend.

Just like that, Jean said. Over.

Yes, said Mariel. Just like that. The way it happens sometimes.

Sad, said Jean.

Yup.

It really is sad, Jean said. But at least, at least, what there is out of it all, is this little chip of humanity.

And she nodded at the pram.

Little chip of humanity? Wow. Mariel laughed. That's very profound, Jean.

They walked past shop after shop, and when they were waiting at the traffic lights Mariel said, The thing I should say, Jean—and this is the thing that Malcolm does not feel the same way about—the thing I should say is that I intend to go home. Back to Canada.

Jean had said that no, she couldn't be serious.

But Mariel was and she had numerous reasons, including the fact that her mother wasn't well. And that her long-term employment prospects were better over there. And that her plan had never been to stay for any length of time in Ireland.

But what about Malcolm? Was she going to take Anton away from him, take him away just like that?

Mariel pulled at her ponytail. She said that it wasn't something that was easy to do but it was for the best.

The best for who? Jean said.

My mother's not well, she had said again, and she's got no one else.

It had started to rain and everything around was ugly, the people with their hangdog faces, the screaming signs, things reduced, prices cut. Jean might have said, there's me too. There's me. There is me.

But they walked along in dismal silence, until Jean eventually offered the idea that perhaps it might not be forever. You never know, she said, you could always come back after a couple of months. Things might improve. Sometimes they do. And Mariel didn't contradict her, colluding in the fiction that this was something temporary.

It went to the family court. Malcolm did not give consent to the relocation. But the judge found in favour of the mother, as was usual. He was to have access during holidays, but his one trip to Canada had been a disaster. Anton was strange with him. He cried when he was passed into Malcolm's arms. And then there was the near punch up with the guy who Mariel said was one of her co-workers.

\*

Malcolm had found the picture that he had been looking for earlier. Look, he said, this is her.

The young woman was on a beach, grinning at the camera as she stood on one leg in a balletic pose.

Yoga, said Malcolm.

She looks very nice.

Really into yoga and all of that. Not the spiritual guff, chakras and all that crap, just the exercise.

She certainly looks very well.

Jean still walked the same route up one side of the road and down the other even though Mariel and Anton had left almost two years ago. The Indian restaurant had gone out of business and the bar had supposedly caught fire. The chinaware shop that had held on for so long was no longer there and in its place there was a shop that sold bodybuilding supplements. There was a new estate agent's, three by three photos of new houses in the window. There was a new chemist's shop. W7 was in there at the W7 stand. W7 was a budget make-up brand, one of a number that ran the length of the shop. W7 stood with the usual diamante bag but at close range Jean could see that some of the glass pieces had fallen off, loose threads hanging where they used to be attached. She never wore trainers like Black Sail or pumps like Inakeen. W7 always had heels. W7 was putting eyeshadows on the back of her hand, dark greens, purples, browns, bruise-like colours. Jean considered the Maybelline jumbo mascaras at the next stand, the blue and blackest black, the almost black, while W7 moved on to liquid eyeliners, drawing a repeated figure of eight on her wrist with one of the tiny brushes. Jean could see the weave of her scarf, the warp and weft, and the points of the pins that she had used to secure it. W7 was wearing trousers and even though they were dark Jean could see the inch or two at the hem where she had walked in water. W7 dropped an eyeliner and Jean bent down to pick it up. W7 took it, smiled and put it back.

I don't suppose you want something to eat do you, Malcolm? Jean asked. Maybe you'd like to stay and have some tea? It'd be good if you did. I did a shop yesterday so there's some nice stuff.

No, he said. Gonna be heading on before too long. Just a flying visit really.

Right you are then.

Did Mariel mention me?

Jean couldn't remember.

Did she mention me, say anything?

Of course she did, Jean said.

Maybe I should go back again to the court. Try to get some real ballbreaker who's going to make things a nightmare for her.

Christ knows the ideas that kid's going to get, he went on. Give it another year and he won't even know who in the name of God I actually am, that's if he even knows now.

Mariel and Anton might move back at some point, Jean said.

Oh aye right, like anybody believes that.

You need to go over again maybe next summer. I'm sure it would be better than last time.

Yeah how dead on of Mariel, generously giving me an opportunity to see my own son.

Jean was silent.

Well, anyway, like I said, flying visit.

Do you know what, before you go, would you mind having a look upstairs? Jean asked. I'm trying to sort things out a bit. There's a couple of boxes of stuff in your room. I wouldn't want to throw anything away that you would like to keep.

Like I should be grateful for the opportunity to see my own son.

He shook his head. Let's see this stuff then.


Jean became so accustomed to the schedule over the road: it was one of the certainties of life that W7 left early in the morning and came back in the afternoon, carrying the bag that probably contained a laptop computer. Most days, at about half past eleven, Inakeen and Black Sail would leave the house, sometimes on foot, sometimes in the car. Sometimes they would bring back shopping, sometimes nothing at all. On Fridays they would all leave at afternoon teatime and come back in the evening.

The curtains were always opened in strict order: the two upstairs bedrooms which Jean took to be Inakeen's and W7's, then the downstairs. Jean thought that Black Sail would have taken the room at the back, grumping because it was the smallest, but really being quite pleased because it got the sun in the afternoon and looked out onto the back garden. Jean could tell who was opening the curtains: if it was W7 then she was actually visible because she came in front of the curtains to pull them, whereas Inakeen was never seen. Black Sail was invisible too, but Jean could tell it was her the way they were yanked open. One morning last month the curtains in the one of the upstairs bedrooms remained closed, and they stayed that way for the next two days. And then after that the other bedroom curtains also stayed closed. Jean thought that they were ill. She took a walk down the parallel road to see their house from the back, and she could see that the curtains were closed in the back room too. She wondered if she should do something and eventually decided to hang on their front door a bag containing a loaf of bread and two pints of milk. When she went over, she rang the bell which gave an unlikely peal of extended complexity. Jean touched the leaves of one of Inakeen's plants at the door as she listened to hear footsteps—but there were none. In the morning the bag was still there. Should she take it back? Jean waited until midday and then went over to retrieve it. It had been raining and water had pooled in the folds of the bag. As she passed their living room she peered in the window. There was a big sofa, soft looking, corduroy perhaps, and stuff all over the floor, magazines and shoes. She imagined the three of them, laughing at something, feet up on the sofa. The next day Jean was pleased to see that the curtains were opened again in the front room on the right, and then W7 appeared with the laptop bag. It took a little longer for Inakeen to get over whatever it was because her curtains stayed closed for another few days.

Inakeen didn't mean mum however. That had been an unexpected revelation. The previous month, Jean went to the doctor's because she had reached the age when she could get the free flu jab. She felt obliged to go because they had sent her a letter. The waiting room was full. Each time the buzzer was pressed so that someone could gain admittance all heads turned to gawp. The woman who tried to get through the door with the double buggy caused a stir, and the man in the yellow jacket with a bandage over one eye. Jean was astonished to see W7 appear. Like before, people looked at her and then at each other for a moment before going back to reading the cheap magazines or watching the television. If only it had been Black Sail who stormed in, in full regalia, her eyes going what? what? you got a problem? That would have been something. But W7 didn't join everyone in the waiting room; she went behind the counter to speak to one of the receptionists, and then from what Jean could see, she moved to the doctors' area.

The practice nurse who gave her the injection said that they had been busy that morning. When those letters went out there was always an influx.

But anyway, the woman nurse said. Makes the day go quick.

Jean rolled down the sleeve of her blouse.

She tried to sound amused. And I see you've even got the women in the headscarves coming in.

What's that?

One of those women with the headscarves.

Oh, the nurse said. Yes. That wee girl. That wee girl's the Somali interpreter. We need to get them in now you see. There's different interpreters come in on different mornings.

I see.

The way of it nowadays. There'll be a good few Somali patients in soon.

Changed times, Jean said.

As she passed the reception on the way out, she saw that W7 was there, gathering up some medical records.

Excuse me, Jean said. Excuse me.

W7 looked up and Jean saw her winged eyeliner.

I just wanted to say—

What is it, love? said the receptionist, coming over.

Oh, just that, I don't have to pay, do I?

Course you don't, love. Free for the over sixty-fives.

When she got home Jean went to the computer and typed in Inakeen. Somali—translation to—English. It didn't mean mother. It didn't mean mum. It meant 'let's go.' But Inakeen was Inakeen now anyway; Jean wasn't going to come up with something new and Inakeen suited her.

I just wanted to say that I live across the road from you.

Nothing upstairs that I want other than this. Dad got me this. He held up a deflated rugby ball. Chuck the rest out.

Right you are, said Jean.

Pisses me off big time that dad never got to meet his grandson.

Yes, Jean said. But not much we can do about it.

A real, real pity. Don't think he would have thought much of all this Canada shit. Wonder what he would have made of it.

Might have thought it wasn't ideal.

Don't think he'd have liked Mariel much. Don't know why I liked Mariel much.

So, Malcolm said, who won?

Who won what?

That thing you were going on about. The competition. You know, the thing that you ended up being a non-starter in.

Oh that, Jean said. Well, there were highly commended pictures, quite a lot of them, and then third prize was, third prize was an old cottage in Donegal. And then second was of a close up of an old man's face, a profile, and then first was Carrick Castle. A woman at Carrick Castle, taken by somebody from my club. The club I used to go to.

Woman at Carrick Castle, said Malcolm. Sounds crap. That was the winner?

On the camera club trip to Carrick Castle, Jean was given a lift by Sam the tutor, along with Angie, the divorcee. The two of them sat in the front and Jean in the back. Jean listened as Sam talked about his work at the art college. His wife worked there too. Angie had just been promoted to a new grade in the civil service. All change. Angie's stilettos had complex lacing, probably not best for castle cobbles and winding steps. Jean had seen them as Angie walked towards the car. Angie had problems with her camera. Could Sam help her? Jean saw through the gap in the car seats the sheen of Angie's knee and how Sam's hand was only a small stretch away from it. They hardly remembered her in the back. When Jean caught Sam's eyes in the rear-view mirror she knew he saw only the retreating white lines of the road.

It was well composed, Jean said. Good enough photo, I suppose.

The winning entry had been a crisp study of the girl in the white dress, taken against the brick of an interior wall. She remembered the half-circle of photographers.

Anyway you won't see me for a bit, Malcolm said. I got a lot of work on next week and then because I've still got holiday time left, I'm going to try to get away for a few days. Might even head over to Scotland. I'll just see how it goes. Would quite like to head over to Scotland.

That's fine, said Jean. Hope you have a good time, if you decide to go away.

Malcolm said that he had joined a new gym. He was going to head on down to it for a quick session. Given up on the other place, he said. The new one down in Hill Street didn't have a membership fee so it worked out better value. He said that that was another thing that he didn't like about the new boss, always eating, probably in the category of obese. Eating all the time.

When Jean was waving goodbye as Malcolm drove off, she saw the flashing blue light of the television in the house across the road. They would all be in that living room, on the sofa, nested in corduroy. Inakeen was probably a good cook, the kitchen warm with simmering stews. They would have kicked their shoes off. When Jean went back into her living room she switched off the television and let the silence settle. She had half a thought to ring Mariel—if she could speak to Anton or Mariel, just hear a few words—but it was afternoon for them and there was never any answer at that time, whatever they were doing.

Jean climbed the stairs to Malcolm's room. She took a seat on his bed. That stuff in the boxes wasn't even worth taking to the charity shop. Old cassettes and videos, ancient textbooks never returned, a glass bottle filled with one pence pieces, nobody wanted it. Jean ran her hand along the duvet, black faded to grey in places with the sun. She undid the poppers of the cover, half of them missing anyway, and pulled it off. The duvet looked lumpy with clumped feathers.

Downstairs Jean laid the duvet cover across the kitchen table. There were so many chairs in the house: the three-piece suite, the four chairs around the kitchen table, the same number around the dining room table. The duvet cover was too long by at least a foot and a half. She was only five foot four. Jean got out the good scissors and cut with a steady, firm hand. She judged where to make the short, horizontal cut, about seven inches from the top, and the point of the scissors went through the fabric neatly.

Outside it was still and there was no one about, no one

to see Jean cross the road. She could see perfectly well through the aperture; the slit had been cut in just the right place. From the other side of the road she saw her own house looked tired. Jean lifted her covered hand to ring the bell, and this time, through the grandiose chime, she hoped she could hear footsteps.

Inakeen, she would say. Let's go.

# Observation

Thing about people like her, people like Kim Cassells, is that they think they're something special. Cath's mum was ironing a shirt, pinching the sleeve at the shoulder and cuff to crisp the line. And they're not. She put down the iron, did the other sleeve. Cath wanted to hear more. What way do you mean? Well, her mum said, people like that think the world owes them something but it owes them nothing at all and it couldn't give two hoots about their pretty face or the pretty face they used to have. That this was how the world felt about things sounded a source of some satisfaction.

Kim Cassells was Cath's friend Lauren's mum. She was always that, Kim Cassells, never just plain Kim. Lauren had to do her own washing. Doesn't take a genius to turn a dial was what Kim Cassells said. One time when Lauren and Cath were in town, Lauren said she needed to buy new bedding. Where would you even get something like that? Cath asked. Loads of places, Lauren said. You just haven't a clue. She needed a fitted sheet and had to explain to Cath what a fitted sheet actually was. ChipChop in town was where they always went for something to eat. They kept each other up to date with the latest capers of the desperadoes from school, their different schools where there were the same characters: the aspiring hard man, the girl who was bisexual—no gay—no bisexual, the person who was always spreading rumours. One day in ChipChop, when school had been exhausted, the talk turned to Kim Cassells. There was a crowd of boys there that day, occupied with downloading porn ringtones to their phones. They kept ringing each other so that they could hear the elaborate crescendo of female gasping. Lauren said that there was a new boyfriend on the scene for her mum. That wasn't anything particularly unusual because Kim Cassells had had many boyfriends in the time since Lauren and Cath had been friends. One of them had been an estate agent, another an accountant. Then there was a local footballer; a photo of the two of them at the launch of a pre-mixed vodka drink had been in the paper. She was always out on the town for a meal on Valentine's night with somebody or other. Valentine's night in town, Cath's dad said, was only for mugs hoping to get their end away.

Yeah, Lauren said. This new guy is called Stuart. What's he look like? Cath asked. Lauren shrugged. Alright. He's just a guy. He's around our place all the time. She closed the lid on her cardboard box of noodles. I'm going to eat the rest of this later. He's a bit younger than some of the others. Twenty-six. Cath said that that wasn't really crazy young. Well nearer my age than hers, Lauren said. She pushed the noodle box on the tray that was sitting on the table. I'm stuffed after these, I can't eat any more. Maybe let's just go, Cath said. Cos I've just about had enough of these ringtones.

Kim Cassells met Stuart at her local gym. That she was an exercise enthusiast was obvious from even a quick consideration of her physique. Being in proximity to Kim Cassells had always made Cath feel lumpen. She had various accoutrements that she used at home to supplement her workouts at the gym and most evenings she went for a run. She had white tubs of protein supplements lined up in the kitchen and in the living room there were kettlebells of varying weights. If she went on holiday it was to places where the hotel complex had a gym. Kim Cassells always went on holiday with friends and Lauren was farmed out to someone or other. They were adults-only resorts: Kim Cassells wasn't slogging for a year to spend a week listening to other people's screaming kids.

When they got off the bus on the way home, Lauren said that there was something she wanted to tell Cath that was highly confidential. Cath had heard this before. A lot of expectation was generated, but invariably the info was something totally banal. It was always easy to keep highly confidential something that no person was interested in knowing anyway. Well, Lauren said, it's Stuart. Your mum's guy? Yeah, she said. Well, thing is, I've kissed him and stuff. Right, Cath replied. Wow. She was pretty interested in the *and stuff*. Is he good looking? Like, is he really hot? Lauren considered. Well, not celebrity hot, but normal person quite hot. He's nearer my age than hers. Cath didn't say, you've told me that already. It was just one of those things, totally unplanned, Lauren said. She was going down the stairs and he was going up the stairs and she moved to the side to let him pass and he moved to the side too at exactly the same time and they both laughed the way you do when that happens and then he put his hand on the back of her head—she showed Cath where—and he pulled her towards him and then that was that. Lauren said she was wearing her dressing gown. Cath had seen that dressing gown. It was patterned like a carpet and it had a hood. I had nothing on underneath, she said. Because I'd just had a shower. They were now outside Lauren's house. So then what happened after? Did you continue going down the stairs and he continued going up? Yes, said Lauren. Because he was heading to the toilet. And I was going to get a glass of water. What about your mum? Cath asked. What if she finds out?

The majority of guys, Cath thought later, if they were offered a night with Kim Cassells or Lauren would pick Kim Cassells, on account of her being really very good looking. That was what she reckoned although her knowledge of guys was pretty theoretical. Lauren might be a much more pleasant person and not at all sour like her mum, but pleasantness in the short term might not actually account for much. Kim Cassells or Lauren though, maybe it was a mistake to assume an either/or. Perhaps the answer was that fellas would pick both, like this guy Stuart, if it could be arranged. Cath kept looking at her dad who was over in the armchair; she was trying to see him afresh, wondering if anyone from school would find him attractive. Perhaps if he was a millionaire, a billionaire that would clinch it, but without the lure of dirty cash she didn't think he would do it for anybody. His sideburns shaded from brown to white, and the grey jogging bottoms he had started to wear around the house were over-elasticated at the ankles, in the style of a comfortable genie.

Dad, did you actually have many girlfriends before you got married? Cath asked. I can't remember, he said. Of course you can. Have a think. Before you were married: did you have many girlfriends? He reconsidered. No. I didn't. Maybe I should have had. Why are you asking? Cath said that she just wondered. Well, I didn't, he said. I met your mother and then boom. He didn't say boom with much enthusiasm. Her dad was concentrating on the film on the telly. There was a woman with long brown hair contemplating something at a desk. Do you think she's good looking? Cath asked. She's alright, he said. I think she's not too bad.

When Cath went upstairs to go to bed, there was no need to go down again but she did, so that she could stop on the stairs. She tilted her head, imagining a figure on the step below who was still tall enough to tower over her. She put her hand to the back of her head and opened her mouth slightly. What are you doing? It was her dad at the bottom of the stairs. What are you looking at? he said. Nothing. It's just I thought I could see a crack in the ceiling. The ceiling? You serious? He took the stairs two at a time to peer at smooth white plaster. No, he said. There's no crack in the ceiling. You must be seeing things.

Under the pretext of needing a jumper she had lent her some months ago, Cath called round to Lauren's house because she was interested in getting a look at Stuart. Crap, you need that jumper, hope I can find it, Lauren said as she went upstairs. Although the television was on, there was no one in the living room. One of the kettlebells was in the middle of the rug. Cath went over and gave it a swing. There hadn't been anyone in the kitchen either. Maybe Stuart didn't come around until later on or maybe he wasn't coming at all. There was nothing to indicate his presence, no empty coat on one of the kitchen chairs, no sports bag in the hall. Kim Cassells' car had been in the driveway, but there was no sign of her either, other than a pair of lycra leggings hung over the banister. When Cath held them up, she saw they were three-quarter length. Then the bathroom door opened and Kim Cassells emerged, wrapped in a towel. Hi, Cath said. Kim Cassells' skin was still wet. Cath could see the beads of water on her shoulders. On her arm there was a round dent from that injection people used to get. She had a tattoo of some text on her shoulder and when she turned Cath was able to read it. *Only God Can Judge Me.* She was a badass and mortal opinion was of no interest to her.

Lauren, Kim Cassells said. My hairdryer. Where is it?

Lauren dashed to her room to retrieve the hairdryer with the flex neatly wrapped around it. Sorry, she said. I borrowed it the other morning. I should have left it back.

Cath sat on the bed as Lauren looked for the jumper she didn't care if she ever saw again. Lauren had plastic boxes of clothes under her bed and some old Christmas decorations, tinsel and a miniature fibre-optic tree. She put bits and pieces up in her room because Kim Cassells took a minimal approach to Christmas. The hairdryer in the next room suddenly switched up a gear. There was only that wall between Lauren and Kim Cassells. In the houses in Kim Cassells' street the walls were thin, just plasterboard. Kim Cassells' room was lilac and grey, Cath had seen it from the landing.

What's everyone up to this evening? Cath asked.

Lauren said that they were going for a drink in some new place.

Who's they?

My mum and Stuart obviously, she said. Hey! Found it! And Lauren pulled the jumper from one of the plastic boxes. It's in a state, she said.

Doesn't matter at all, Cath replied. No worries at all.

Lauren said she needed to get on with some work. That new woman always gives us stuff for the next day. This jumper, Cath said, it's actually pretty useful. Goes with a lot of stuff. Sorry it's in a state, Lauren said. I was wondering, Cath began, can you actually iron wool, or is that not what you do, don't know, don't know if this is actually even wool, could be something else. Cath, I really don't know, Lauren said. Then the doorbell rang. The doorbell! Cath kept on looking for the tag of the jumper even though she had already seen it and that the jumper was polyamide/ acrylic/viscose blend. The doorbell rang again. On the infrequent occasions when Cath came around, she never went in the front. She always went round the back of the house where the door was usually open.

Get that, Lauren! Kim Cassells shouted. I'm still putting on my make-up! Get it would you!

Lauren put down the book she was holding and went down the stairs with Cath following her. Beyond the pebbled glass of the front door was an amorphous white and blue shape. Lauren! Kim Cassells shouted again. Lauren turned the lock and to Cath's surprise ran back up the stairs again, leaving her standing there in front of the door that was only ajar. The person outside, the person who Cath hoped was Stuart, didn't move to push the door open. Cath waited for a few seconds and then decided that she needed to take the handle and pull it open. She did this slowly, and what was in front of her was a man of about six feet tall in black jeans and a T-shirt. Had he just had a haircut? His parting was shaved in to one side. Cath looked down at his trainers which were pristine apart from a black smudge where the leather met the sole on the right hand toe. It wasn't the warmest of evenings, but he had no jacket.

Hi, Cath said.

He gave a quick nod. Alright?

Yes, Cath said. I'm just a friend.

Okay, Stuart said.

Just to let you know that you are at the right place okay, Cath said.

Yeah I know, Stuart said.

Cath realised she hadn't opened the door sufficiently to allow him to come in, so she took a step back and pulled it wide, pressing herself against the wall so that he had ample space to enter into the hall. And then Kim Cassells was coming down the stairs with neat little steps. She was wearing a short blue dress and cork wedges, and a jacket that looked leather but was actually some kind of laminated fabric; Cath knew that because it brushed against her when Kim Cassells put her arms around Stuart's neck and kissed him. Cath moved further back. Stuart had both arms around Kim Cassells' waist but then his hand moved to bunch up the flimsy blue fabric and Cath could see a couple of inches of bare ass. Am I late? Stuart eventually said. No, but I'm glad to see you, Kim Cassells replied. And then she noticed that Cath was there. What are you doing? she said. Why are you standing there? Cath said, I'm standing here, Kim, because I came down to open the door when you were drying your hair. A couple of weeks ago she wouldn't have spoken to Kim Cassells like that. She said she was leaving now anyway and she shouted goodbye to Lauren. Halfway home Cath realised she'd left the jumper.

They had moved Cath to the till in her part-time job which was good in some ways because the smell of the chicken rotisserie in her old spot, the deli section, clung to her clothes. But the shop felt too vast at times, a metal barn, when there weren't enough customers, and she was sitting at the till. The orange lettering across her chest was crude and she had to wear a baseball cap.

The old school caretaker bought a lot of dog food. There was a woman who used to teach French who always made a joke about how much wine was in her trolley. It was the only place in the area really where people could do their main shop. Earlier on in the evening, when Kim Cassells and Stuart appeared in Cath's queue, a bird had flown into the shop. It flapped from one corner of the roof to the other, too high for anyone to catch it. Bloody stupid thing, the supervisor said, and there'll be shit all over the top of those shelves. It flew hard into the wall and dropped down dead.

Oh it's you, Kim Cassells said. I didn't know you worked here.

I didn't know I worked here either, Cath said. I just found myself sitting at this till, which was all very weird, very weird indeed.

Kim Cassells said nothing and put the remainder of her shopping on the conveyor belt. The cold white light flattered absolutely no one. Cath thought of a broken Kinder egg when she looked at Kim Cassells' two-tone hair, greasy brown at the roots, white at the tips. As she bent over the trolley, her necklace with two dice on it dangled off her chin.

Hi, Cath said to Stuart. I'm the person that opened the door to you the other night. You know, before you went out for a drink.

Stuart did a little performance of pretending that the question of Cath's identity had been on his mind and that it was a relief to have it revealed. Yeah, Cath said. I'm Lauren's friend.

Kim Cassells started speaking to him in a voice too low for Cath to hear. She looped her arm around his waist and hooked a finger on one of the belt rings of his jeans. The final few things went through, some washing-up liquid, a loaf of bread, and a rolled-up pack of bin bags.

What are you up to this evening, anything exciting? Cath asked.

Kim Cassells had her bag open for her purse.

No, why are you doing something exciting this evening? she said.

Not sure, Cath replied. See how it goes. Night's still young.

Being annoying was a lot of fun. Kim Cassells couldn't find her purse.

Don't worry Kim, Cath said. Just you take your time, I'm just like that too, I can never find anything.

When Kim Cassells eventually handed over her card she asked where the bags were. I said I needed bags. She hadn't asked for bags but Cath pulled out a flurry of them. So sorry there you are, she said. There were the cheap bags and then there were more substantial ones, twenty pence dearer. Stuart ripped one of the cheap bags as he tried to separate the ends of it. Oh let me get you another one, Cath said. Stuart gave a nod goodbye, but Kim Cassells didn't look in Cath's direction. As they walked off Cath saw that a pen was stuck in Stuart's back pocket, a blue biro.

Next time Lauren and Cath were in ChipChop, it wasn't the usual dance hits being played, it was actually Chinese music. It's making the food taste different, Cath said. Do you know what I mean? Making it taste better. Cath was waiting to hear about Stuart. So, she said. So what? Well? she said. Well what? You know fine rightly well what. Come on, how's it going? How's what going? Lauren said. Oh wise up, Lauren, don't get on like a dick. Lauren gave a long sigh. So what does that mean? Cath said, but Lauren just shrugged. She looked into the middle distance and then down to the side, then over to the door. She tucked her hair behind her ear and bit her lip.

She'd parted her hair differently from usual, and the lipstick she was wearing was a new colour, not quite coral, not quite pink. She reckons she's beautiful now, Cath thought. Because she's got some random guy, she thinks she's beautiful. He's probably told her, you're beautiful.

Well, Lauren said, and sighed again. Cath lifted the bottle of soy sauce to read the label. Naturally Brewed Soy Sauce. 250 ml. Over 300 years of excellence. On the back there was the nutritional information.

It's going alright, Lauren said. And do you know what, he's going to take me out for driving lessons, well driving practice, it's not like he's an instructor.

Carbohydrates of which sugars. Fat of which saturates.

So, Cath said, you had sex with him yet or not? Lauren said yes, the other day. The other day? Where? She said that it was in the house. She was home early and he came around. She said she wasn't worried about her mum turning up. Why not? Because she was at work. Listen, Lauren said, they're not married or anything, they haven't even been seeing each other that long. I know but still, Cath said, it's not a good idea, she could throw you out. I can take care of myself, Lauren said. Done it for years.

On a trip to the cinema with Lauren's friends from school everyone disagreed about which film to see so the group split between three screens. Cath went with a boy and girl she'd never met before and they all chipped in for a giant Coke and a popcorn. Although the popcorn was beside her, the Coke was in the holder two seats away. After asking for it three times, she didn't want to ask for it again. There was something wrong with the popcorn. It was far too salty, and there were too many shots of landscapes in the film. It wasn't very interesting and in the dark she might as well have been by herself.

Back at the house, Kim Cassells was on the sofa with a glass of wine and a magazine. She was wearing silky looking sports shorts and fluffy slippers. Cath wondered if her tan was fake or sunbed. Why are you two back? Kim Cassells said, switching on the telly with the remote. Thought you'd be round her place. She nodded in Cath's direction. No, Cath said. They've got people there tonight. They're busy. Cath's staying the night here, Lauren said. Oh is she? Switch the immersion on would you, Lauren? Kim Cassells said, I want to have a bath. She stretched out her legs and then curled them up under her again. Stuart not around this evening? Cath asked. Kim Cassells scanned the room, pretending to look for him. Nope, doesn't seem to be. She tossed the magazine to the floor. You two not find any nice young fellas in town? No? It wasn't really that type of night, Lauren said. No, what type of night was it then? It was a low key night, Cath said.

The dressing gown was hanging on the hook on Lauren's door, in the weak light looking like the rear view of the grim reaper. Cath was on a sleeping bag on Lauren's floor, her head half under a desk. She pushed the bin full of damp cotton wool and wet wipes a bit further away from her. Is your mum's tan fake or does she go to sunbeds or is she just naturally really brown? Cath asked. Oh sunbed, Lauren said. Naturally really brown, you got to be having a laugh. Place down the road, turbo beds, you not heard about it, man got done for spying on people through keyholes cos they're all lying in the nude, who'd want to look, guy must've been desperate. I'm turning the light off, Lauren said. The sleeping bag smelt smoky, because maybe it had been used for an expedition where they cooked over open fires, out on a mountaintop with a mist coming down, surrounded by gaping stretches of nothing, but here there was a desk and a chest of drawers Cath could touch with her feet, the thin walls, and another room nearby. She pulled the sleeping bag up around her face. The red display of the alarm clock changed an eight to a nine and all it took was the removal of two little lines. There was the sound of the immersion heater cooling down.

It was 3.32 when Cath woke up to a soft knocking, a sound which crept away as swiftly as it appeared. It was probably the central heating ticking to a standstill, a branch blowing against the window. But was there even a tree in the back garden? There was a washing line, but not a tree. Cath propped herself up against the desk. The sound now had another layer, a human dimension, and it was Kim Cassells. Cath's eyes were readjusting and she could make out the outline of one of Lauren's posters, the hood of the dressing gown. She couldn't hear anything from Stuart, but there was Kim Cassells. Then a light went on and a yellow wedge cut into the darkness of the room. Somebody was going to the toilet, possibly Stuart from the sound of the footsteps. Cath wasn't sure, but it looked like Lauren had her pillow over her head. Lauren, Cath said. There was a flush and then the light went off and the house settled back to where it was before. They would be lying with their arms around each other now.

Those things in the light were motes and, rarer than rainbows, you only got to see them now and again: fibres from Lauren's jumpers, Kim Cassells' hoodies, flakes of skin, tiny particles of paper, the white dust of dry shampoo, the icing sugar from the buns they ate one time, all moving slowly in the narrow beam of morning light between the curtains. This house was full of the stuff and they all bathed in it. Last night Cath had lain in the dark for ten minutes after the flush of the toilet before getting up herself. The condom with a knot in it floating in the pan looked kind of small and forlorn. She hadn't wanted Lauren to come across it so she had lifted it out.

Downstairs Stuart had no top on and he was frying bacon. He had a tea towel hanging from his back pocket. You girls after any of this? he asked. Don't mind, Cath said, if you've got enough to go around, but Lauren shook her head and took a seat at the table. They weren't the same jeans that Stuart had on that day when he was with Kim Cassells doing the shopping. The pockets were lower down and these ones concertinaed around his ankles a little more, although they weren't baggy as such. Across his back there were little mauve flecks, faded acne scars from how long ago, ten years maybe? There was dance music on the radio and he nodded his head to it as he moved the bacon around the pan. Put on a bit of toast there, Lauren, would you? he said. Put it on yourself. I'm not having any bacon. Oh right, Stuart said, so not having bacon prevents you from putting on any toast? Cath said, No worries, I'll do it. Stuart stared at the open cupboard. You guys not got any sauce around here? The cupboard was fairly bare, an old shortbread tin, some cans, a couple of jars. Kim Cassells favoured low-cal ready meals. Where's all your sauce? he asked. Lauren went to another cupboard that had bowls, plates, saucers, a plastic dispenser of sweeteners for tea, a jar of honey and a bottle of something. She put down reduced sugar barbecue sauce on the worktop beside him. Sauce, she said. He lifted it up and looked at it. Don't know whether to bother with that. He put it down again. Well then don't, said Lauren, you were the one who was wanting sauce, not anyone else. If you don't want it, fine.

Cath had put on the sweatshirt that she'd been wearing the day before. Lauren was still in her jammy top, a T-shirt with a scoop neck. Cath couldn't remember noticing before how rounded Lauren's tits were. In the action of reaching for a newspaper that was sitting on the far side of the table, they shifted under the soft fabric and there was a line of horizontal stretch from one nipple to the other. When Lauren stood up, Cath thought it was to get the toast, but instead she slid her arms around Stuart. He jumped in surprise and then when he turned around Lauren started trying to kiss him.

What are you doing? he said. Stop that for fuck's sake. Jesus Christ. He peeled her off, an arm at a time. Wise up, Lauren, he said and looked over at Cath.

Oh, don't be worrying about Cath for God's sake. Cath knows all about absolutely everything.

Well, no, Cath said, I don't know all about absolutely everything.

Well, stop it, Stuart said. I mean it. Cut it out.

He put a couple of slices of bacon on a plate and passed it over to Cath, while Lauren stared at him. He said nothing and she kept on staring. What? he said. What? He sat down at the table. Now where's the knives and forks? he said. Where's the fucking knives and forks in this house? Christ almighty. Although there was plenty of room for Lauren to get past between the units and the table she knocked hard into his shoulder.

Sorry! she said.

As Lauren went up the stairs she must have met Kim Cassells coming down. Hey, Kim Cassells said when she came into the kitchen. Stuart had found the drawer with the knives and forks because he was holding a bunch of them. Kim Cassells went over and put her hand on his arm. Babes, she said. Then she slipped her hand in the back pocket of his jeans. The skinny strap of her top separated *Judge Me* from *Only God Can*. Kim Cassells took the seat where Lauren had been. Oh so you're still here, she said to Cath. Where'd you sleep, on the floor? Yeah, Cath said. It was fine. No problem. Kim Cassells got a jar from the cupboard. She put a spoonful of white powder into a glass of water and it turned bright green. That's some colour, Cath said. Kim Cassells took a seat again. As she sipped her drink, she started talking to Stuart about a woman she knew from the gym. She said that Stuart knew her too, but he couldn't remember. She kept explaining her in more detail, where she lived, what she did, but he didn't recall her. But she's the woman who's always doing leg presses. The one with the blue and pink striped top. He didn't know. Kim Cassells then began telling him about a holiday that this woman had gone on with her boyfriend, which was for couples only and everyone slept in individual round lodges at the end of separate jetties. It's basically paradise, she said. Just couples, she added. You look out and all you see is the sea. Can you imagine? The low fat barbecue sauce tasted of boiled sweets and matches. There was an untouched pool of it on Stuart's plate. He said, I knew a fella went on a holiday like that once, was his honeymoon actually. Alright for the first day, fair enough, the water and all that, but then there's nothing to do, just staring out, it's depressing, so by the third day he was away on over to the staff quarters to play poker with the ones who were working there. And, Stuart said, he still keeps in touch with some of them guys. But is he still married? Cath asked. Oh shit no, packed that in a while ago.

Later in the week, at the end of the first shift at her new job in town, Lauren called around to Cath's. She had got a job in the place that had recently opened that sold cheap, sleek things, notebooks, jugs, bags, picture frames. The uniform was grey with a little mandarin collar. Look what I bought you with my first staff discount, Lauren said. It was a mug in a slate colour. Very nice, Cath said. Don't know if I really need a mug though. It was just something to buy, Lauren said. I'll maybe give it to my mum. Yeah, cool, Cath said. A mug'll make up for the fact you're having sex with her fella. Ha ha, Lauren said. Kim Cassells had suggested that Stuart move in with her, but he wasn't enthusiastic at all. And, anyway, Lauren said, who says it's just sex? Who's saying that?

Haven't seen her in a while, Cath's mum said when Lauren left. Well she's been busy with stuff, hasn't she? School work and a new job and all that. And I hear Kim Cassells is running around with a fella young enough to be her son, her mum said. Don't come into the room here, I'm going to start bleaching the floor. Good luck to her with the latest one because, let's face it, he's not going to work out any better than the rest, the husband was the best of a bad bunch but that's a long time ago. She was on the road the other day, Kim Cassells, Cath's dad said. You didn't mention it, her mum said. Why would I mention it? Why would I mention to you everyone I see? Am I going to tell you about everything? Don't come in, her mum said, there's bleach going on this floor.

Lauren was working on Saturday so they didn't meet in town. ChipChop was going downhill anyway; there was now a To Let sign partially obscuring the name. Lauren said she wasn't too sure if she was going to be home that evening or not, but Cath thought she would call around anyway just to see. She knocked on the back door, but there was no response so she slowly turned the handle. The radio was on in the kitchen, a woman telling some story about something or other. The strip lights under the units flickered slightly. Cath pressed her finger in the wax of the scented candle sitting on the table. How long ago was it lit? The wax still felt soft.

Stuart! came Kim Cassells' voice. Cath could have shouted, no it's me, but she didn't. Stuart? Kim Cassells called again. Cath opened the cupboard. Still just the reduced-sugar barbecue sauce. Down the stairs and into the kitchen and Cath saw how Kim Cassells' smiled faded when she saw it was her. I knocked, Cath said. Well, Lauren's not in, Kim Cassells said. No? Kim Cassells said, no, she's out. What's she up to? Cath asked. She's out getting some driving practice with Stuart, Kim Cassells said. Oh, right, I see. And Cath thought, although she wasn't sure, that Kim Cassells felt a flicker of something. Yes, I'll need to be getting round to that myself, Cath said. Hopefully my dad will take me out too. My dad was saying he saw you the other day. He was saying how well you looked.

# Locksmiths

There was a point when Spanish banks were offering hundred percent mortgages. But the crash came and people couldn't make the payments so bailiffs turned up to repossess homes and locksmiths to change locks. Families stood outside gazing up at their old bedrooms. I read about a woman who bolted the door, ran to an upstairs balcony—and leapt. The guys, the locksmiths, masters of cylinders and springs, had never anticipated that their work would run to this kind of thing. In one of the big cities, the locksmiths said no, that was it, they wouldn't lock people out anymore. Just wouldn't do it.

Early last week I was in the big DIY superstore, getting a few things. All those generators: did many people really need generators? Perhaps they did. A man struggled to carry a huge bag of plaster powder but it dropped and split, sending up a minor mushroom cloud. A call went out over the tannoy for a cleaner. One of the assistants said to me, can I help you, sweetheart? I said, no, all's fine. Because all was fine: I knew what I wanted. I bought a cheap bedside light and a single quilt cover, cotton, the sort that could take a boil wash. I hesitated over the paints with the lovely names, but got the largest tin of pure brilliant white because that would do. In the superstore there was a whole aisle devoted to locks from the basic to the intricate. I got a pack of three towels and a key ring for the extra key I had got cut.

Back when I first got the house I was in here all the time. It was a fairly exciting place. Home improvement, by its nature optimistic. I sometimes spent sixteen, eighteen hours a day working on the house, forgetting to eat. I became acquainted with every bad joist and frame tie. My tool kit grew. I began with a few cheap screwdrivers and moved on to a DeWalt drill, secondhand. I scraped off decades of sticky wallpaper, woodchip giving way to a paisley swirl, paisley swirl yielding to a bottle green paint. It was my gran's house and she left it to me.

If, when I was younger, anyone asked about my mother, the non-specific, 'she's away' seemed to suffice on most occasions. It was rare however that anyone would ask. But had anyone enquired, would there have been a big stigma attached to having a mother in jail? Probably not. At my school there were other people with family members who were in jail or out on licence. In my year, there was Gary whose big brother shot somebody outside a snooker hall. And then in the year above there was Mandy G whose dad beat a woman to death. In all likelihood there were probably others from the years below, but I didn't know about them. You only tended to know about the older kids.

Living with my gran, I watched a lot of soaps and dramas. She always sat in the same seat and smoked; there was a yellow bloom on the ceiling which I eventually with some reluctance painted over. Before each programme my gran would pour herself a whisky and when there was a bar scene she would take a drink because it made her feel that she was there. I'd get a Coke and do the same thing but I was still always in the living room. Everything in the house smelt thick of smoke; it was deep in my school blazer and couldn't be shifted.

The man who was killed by my mother was Tommy Gilmore, an old fella who had hoped, I presume, to spend the remainder of his days recovering from the work accident which had left him incapacitated. He'd got a major pay-out. It was somebody else's carelessness. Those long nights, those longer days, no doubt he looked forward to seeing my mother who called around at first sometimes, and then more frequently. She borrowed money and initially maybe he liked it, the attention she gave him, the prancing and twirling about in the things she had bought, but then when she never paid anything back and only wanted more and more, and when he in turn threatened to contact the police, she beat him with an object, thought to be a poker, although it was never found. Tommy Gilmore had a stroke during the attack but it was the head injuries that killed him.

My gran would visit her daughter every month. It took the best part of a day to get there and back, an elaborate journey involving a bus, a train and a bus. There was a tray we used to call the Chinese tray because it had pictures of dragons on it. On the days when my gran went off, I was left two sandwiches and two glasses of milk on the Chinese tray and told not to answer the front door under any circumstances whatsoever. My gran always came back hobbling because she wore her good shoes.

Twice a year I went with her. It usually coincided with the time when the clocks went back or forward. When we got off the bus we stopped at a cafe near the train station. Anything you asked for in that cafe, they had always just run out of it, but they always let us know this with great regret. That's the last time we're going there, we would say. We're going to take our custom elsewhere. But we kept on going there because it meant that we could continue to see what they had just run out of, just this minute.

After the various security procedures, we took our seats to wait for the women to enter in single file. Some faces lit up at the sight of the visitors. Others' expressions didn't change. My mother's didn't change. The conversational gambits tended to be familiar, more or less. My mother would begin with a litany of grievances which might have included the conduct of certain prison officers or, just as likely, the unavailability of a particular type of sauce. Then my gran would rattle on about characters from the programmes she watched.

Although she had a pretty enough face, my mother was paunchy for a woman, at least most of the time. At one point the prison got refurbed with a new gym with all the latest machines, and when my mother entered the room we saw a pared-down version, alert and hungry. But by the next time the cheekbones had gone. The lustre, clearly, was off the gym.

There were little things. She always had a tissue. She would twist and weave it through her fingers. She did that at least once during every visit and I always watched for it happening. She got a few tattoos on her arms, capital letters, something or other. Her hair looked chewed and the style was permanently eighties despite the passing of the years. On one memorable occasion the two of us sat across the table with exactly the same colour of hair. We had used the same lightening spray which promised golden beach blonde but which reliably turned out orange. That went in the bin when I got home.

The same but sometimes a little different. One time it was obvious that there was something romantic going on with one of the other prisoners; her eyes kept sliding over to a woman on the far side of the room, talking to a guy in a denim jacket. I had watched people giving each other those doleful, burning looks in school. And then there was the time she got religion. For a period my mother wore a cross and a wristband with a Bible verse; she told us about the power of prayer and talked about redemption and her personal relationship with Jesus. She also learned some chords on the guitar.

Yous not believe in Jesus then? she asked us.

As part of a rehabilitation programme, she attended a workshop on education. She had produced some writing which documented her own experience of, and views on, the subject. She said we could read it but the facilitator had collected it in so we couldn't. My mother on that particular visit was very interested in how I was getting on in school. I was quizzed on how I was doing in every class and she was full of motivational advice. On the next trip, I brought my big school file which weighed down my bag on the journey but the conversation never again turned in the direction of education.

My gran died as she had lived, in front of the TV. I found her when I came into the house. I put a cardigan round her, her favourite one, because she had only on a light thing, and I waited until the credits of the programme started rolling before I started making the phone calls. The funeral wasn't large: some neighbours and a few relations who had seen the death notice in the paper. The prison granted my mother leave to attend on compassionate grounds. The short service took place in an old mission hall my gran had attended at some point; the people from the hall picked the hymns and the readings; the only proviso they made was that my mother couldn't be in the hall. That was fine: no objection to that. I did one of the Bible readings, the thing about there being a time for this, a time for that, a time for whatever. My mother appeared only when we arrived at the cemetery. She was standing under a tree with some man and I couldn't recall having seen her outdoors before, although I must have done, when I was younger. She was close to the fella, conspiratorial, but then I saw that she was handcuffed to him. She nodded over to me, a dip of acknowledgement and that was it.

Some people had congregated in the car park and although it was starting to rain they weren't wanting to dash off too quickly. There were a couple of younger fellas who must have been at another funeral and they made a whole deal of taking off their ties, stuffing them in their pockets, opening their top buttons. They passed round a bottle of QC sherry. They were talking to my mother, so I says to him, and he says to me, and I says what the fuck, and he says wait a minute what the. My mother found them very funny. They offered her the sherry and she took it in her free hand while the man handcuffed to her tactfully and serenely looked to the far end of the car park. One of the fellas tipped the bottle when she was drinking and it ran all down my mother's front, down the blue suit somebody must have lent her. She took a drink from the bottle again until I heard the prison guy say, okay, now come on, that's enough. He was right: that was enough. My mother, pulled along at the wrist, tottered back to the car through puddles in heels that didn't fit. The younger fellas gave her a shout as she headed away. When I got home I had a cup of tea on the Chinese tray and watched a bit of a hospital drama.

And so, last weekend it was the first time in years that I was making the journey. After my gran died I didn't visit. Now, instead of travelling by bus, train and bus, I was in a car. I took a detour so that I could see if the cafe that had always just run out was still there, but it was now a phone shop. When I got to the place there were some people waiting outside—a man in a tuxedo holding a red rose, and some kids charging around with pink helium balloons—but others like me just sat in their cars. I wasn't sure what to do. When she appeared I just sat watching her for a while. Not long. Just a minute or two. She looked smaller than I remembered and her hair was back in a ponytail. She had a blue holdall bag. I tooted the horn, but she didn't look over. I tooted it again and then put down the window, shouted over. She looked at me as if to say, oh it's you. I didn't unfasten my seatbelt and I kept on holding the wheel.

On the drive back the car radio was on. She said, what is this? What they going on about? What a load of shit. Talking talking talking. So I turned over to a pop station, but when we hit the roundabout I moved it back again.

She was interested in knowing how long it would take to get home and how fast the car could go. Don't know, I said. I usually don't go any quicker than this. We passed a sign for the big shopping centre that's on the way and she said, Shit I've seen the ads for that place! We going there? We're going there, yeah?

I said, sure. If you want to.

I didn't particularly want to trail round shops so I waited on the seats, gave her twenty-five quid to spend. My mother came back with a skinny belt, a T-shirt with a photo of a sunset on the front and a set of three bracelets.

Back in the car I drove and she fiddled with the bracelets, putting them on one wrist, taking them off, putting them on the other. The belt hadn't been a bargain; the stitching was starting to fray already.

When we got back to the house all was quiet. She said, so there's no party?

She would not have been surprised by a surprise party.

No there's no party, I said.

No one was waiting to jump out and pull a party popper. No one was hiding in the kitchen.

Where's the TV? and she pointed to the spot where the TV would have been years ago. I saw the ghost of the old TV.

I don't have a TV, I said.

She made a slow sucking sound. No TV, she said. She looked at the rows of books.

No TV but.

Here, I said. This is for you. I gave her the key ring out of my bag, a simple grey fake leather fob and a shiny key. Its newly cut teeth felt rough but it had turned with no resistance when I had tried it in the door.

She looked at it and shoved it in the back pocket of her jeans.

That's your front door key, I said.

Yeah, she said. Ta.

Where she had been she wouldn't have had a key. There would have been keys on choke chains, bundles of keys on large metal rings, but none of them would have been in her possession. Perhaps the key on the grey leather fob would have a symbolic value for her.

Don't lose it, I said.

Piss off, she replied.

My mother went up to a room that had once been hers. I could hear the floorboards creak and strain. Maybe she was sitting on the bed thinking about what used to be there; perhaps she was looking out the window at a view not so very different from the one she might remember. Downstairs the clock ticked. I could hear the slight gurgle of the water going into the radiator, the vague bark of that dog two doors down. Then the toilet flushed. The bedroom door closed with a bang. It had been a long time since someone else had been in this house. The air was pounding with so little.

Slow steps brought my mother back to the living room.

Well, she said, flopping onto the sofa, that room is white alright. White, white and white. With a side helping of white.

Window doesn't open properly, she added.

I said that I would have a look at it.

Used to climb out that window, she said. Used to escape out that window.

Where to? I asked.

Anywhere, she said. Wasn't really fussy,

I'd all the posters from the mags on the walls when that was my bedroom, my mother said. You wouldn't have seen the walls for all the pictures.

Who of? I asked. What of?

Can't remember, she said. It was years ago. I was a fuckin teenager.

The walls were cool and smooth now. They weren't

gobbed with Blu-Tack and covered in pictures of leering faces torn out of magazines.

She never knew that I went out, my mother said. She didn't have a clue. Probably because she was half cut herself half the time. Wouldn't have known what was going on, who was in and who was out.

I'd never noticed the clock's tick before. It had a slight reverb.

You had to go out of the window front ways, my mother pointed out. So that you could make the jump to the gutter and then the kitchen roof. One night I wrecked myself.

She pulled up the leg of her jeans to show something.

You see that scar? she asked.

Not really, I said.

There, she pointed.

It was just her skin, white and puckered.

Well I wrecked myself when I fell one time.

If she was so half cut all the time, why did you not just go out the front door and save yourself all of that bother?

Half cut half the time, not all the time, she said. I said half the time.

Easy to get back in, she said, getting back in was alright as long as you stood on the bin to get up onto the kitchen roof. Room was always fuckin freezing, she said, with the window being open all that time.

Well, I said, there's a duvet in the room now. And, as you say, the window doesn't open properly. You won't be getting out the window.

My mother ran her hand down the arm of the sofa. This come from DFS?

I couldn't remember. It might've been there, I said. It was a while ago.

I'd like a leather sofa, she said.

Oh would you? I said.

Yeah, she said. I wouldn't get this. I'd get a leather sofa.

She asked if anyone else lived here.

No, nobody else lives here, I said. Just me.

It's just me since she died, I added.

Just you then.

Just me.

That was one difference, I supposed, among others. There was just me. I wasn't part of a group or a union or a collective. I was on my own. The locksmiths were outside but I was inside. The woman who flew from the balcony they did not know. She was just a name and address on a photocopied list of that day's jobs.

Well it's a dump round here, she said. It was always and I can exclusively reveal to you that it still is. A total fucking dump.

I asked her if she was planning on going somewhere else.

Oh yeah, she said, might well. Got a few ideas. Stuff I got on the go.

Like what? I said.

She tapped her nose to indicate top secret.

Well I'm glad to hear that, I replied. Good.

Yeah it's good, she said.

It's very good, I said. It's very good to hear that you've got stuff on the go. And that you're not stuck in a dump.

You got a fella? she asked.

No, I replied.

Nah didn't think so, she said. What's for the tea?

I had done a big shop before she arrived but there was nothing in the fridge or the cupboards that she wanted. No, no, and absolutely no way. I said that I was a vegetarian.

Oh well you would be, she said. Now why does that not fucking surprise me? Don't be telling me you don't drink either. No booze? You got to be joking.

And she gave a short little laugh. So this is freedom. This is what I've been waiting for. Welcome to the shithole.

My shithole though, I said quietly.

I didn't think she'd heard.

I said it again. My shithole though.

Yeah, she said. I'm sure you'd rob my grave as quick.

Fair's fair, my mother said, you pulled a right fucking smooth move there.

You think so? I said.

There was me waiting on a letter from the law place telling me what I got, she said, there was me waiting to hear what I'd been left. Waiting on a letter that never came. Anyway, fuck the cow.

You got a key, I said.

This room used to have an orange rug, she said. A big orange rug.

I remembered that rug and how I rolled it up to get it out the front door and into the skip.

I'd put my face down on that rug in front of the fire, she said, and it would be like I was lying in the centre of the sun. Right in the very centre of it.

When I was a kid, she added.

I said, Look, do you want me to go down to the off-licence for you? It's only down the road.

She considered but said no, because was the Troubadour still there? Don't tell me the Troubadour's not even there now. I said that it was still there but it was called something different.

Yeah well, beggars can't be choosers, she said. Although it's probably going to be a shithole too.

She went upstairs and came down again wearing the new T-shirt with the sunset.

You coming? she said.

Where to? I asked.

The Troubadour. You've not seen me in, how long? Not even going to go for a drink, how's that meant to make anybody feel? Own flesh and blood, she said.

The Troubadour was fairly empty. My mother had double vodka and Coke and I had an orange juice. Orange juice for fuck's sake, she said.

Coke's flat, she added.

One TV above the bar showed football with no sound and the other female wrestling.

Then my mother shouted out, Geordie!

A small, wiry man had come in. When he saw my mother he let out a yell and held his arms wide. Jesus but would you look who it is! he said. Look who's back! Look at you! When you get out? Hey, son, you going to get this friend of mine a drink?

My mother didn't notice me slip out. I sipped the last of the orange and off I went back home to my house. I read a book for a while, and then I lay upstairs with the light on, listening for the key in my door. I expected my mother, Geordie and various others to come bursting in. The digital display on my bedside clock counted through the hours. The Troubadour hadn't turned out to be such a shithole after all, perhaps. No doubt there had been an after-hours session, a move to another bar, a party back at a house somewhere other than here. There had been other old friends to meet.

The next morning I was up very early. I lay listening but there was nothing. The bedroom, when I ventured to check it, was as was. The white quilt was untouched. There were just a couple of things lying on the floor: her jumper and a pair of knickers. There was no sign of the key so she must have taken it with her. In the bathroom there was her toothbrush in the mug along with mine. I took it out and put it in her blue holdall along with her other bits and pieces, zipped the holdall shut and took it downstairs. I sat on my sofa, which was not leather, and thought for a bit as the wan morning light showed my brushstrokes on the gloss. What I wished was this: that I had a cigarette and a whisky with the ice clinking and that my gran was still here. In the cupboard under the stairs I had my tool kit and I knew I was nothing like the Spanish guys who wouldn't change the locks. The DIY superstore had that whole aisle of mortises and sashes and it opened in less than an hour's time.

# Sweet Home

The name usually given to this type of building—
community centre—was rejected since it was thought
to be pejorative in its suggestion of entrenched cultural
and political ideologies. People's centre, however, was
considered more inclusive so people's centre it was. The
people's centre was being built on waste ground that had
previously been an area for carry-outs, bonfires and, on
one occasion, a dog fight. Before work could start on the
build, effort and resources were dedicated to the removal
of knotweed from the area: the roots of the plants were
injected with large syringes and the foliage was sprayed
with herbicide. And then the steel skeleton of the new
centre was able to rise from the scrub ground until it was
three times taller than any other building in the vicinity.
In the mornings the men working on the site sent the two
youngest for breakfasts in polystyrene boxes from the
nearby cafe. Pneumatic drilling and the clang of metal
didn't entirely drown out the swipes of traffic or the
sometime sound of children at play in the nearby primary
school. The London-based practice, Thanasis, had their
senior architect responsible for the design on site every

month. She stayed in a hotel room in the city centre which, although small, gave her a panoramic view of the place.

The architect who was called Susan Marsh had a husband, Gavin. Originally from Belfast he had left in the early nineteen-eighties to go to university on the mainland where he got a certain mileage out of the time back home when he had been on a bus that got hijacked. His version of events included a lyrical description of the flames. In more recent years, he had made trips to visit his very elderly mother who was in a nursing home in the leafy suburb where he had grown up. He saw a little of the province on these visits. It all seemed very changed from what he remembered, although much of what he remembered was generated by black and white press photography.

Gavin started to accompany Susan on her own trips to Belfast. When she was working he explored the old streets and the new streets, the reclaimed land down at the docks. He visited his mother. Gavin and Susan hired a car and drove the sixty miles to be buffeted raw by the wind coming off the Atlantic. In a harbour bar Gavin complained once again about the slow, clogged travel and predictability to which they had become accustomed at home. It's not as if I need to work in London, he said. And neither, really, do you. Couldn't you get away with only being there a day a week?

From the bar she could see the suck of the tide, its pull. Beaches like that shelved steeply. She could get away without being there at all. The coldness of the water would be a shock at first.

It's a possibility, she said.

Gavin was keen. What was there to keep them, beyond work and their house? And work could be reconfigured and a house could be sold. Susan's parents lived in Scotland but Gavin's mother was in Belfast, or at least a fifteen-minute drive from it. The place had some claim on them, on Gavin at any rate, that London had not. So Susan took charge of selling their old house and buying the new one, and Gavin arranged the removals. Their new house on a grand tree-lined avenue they considered a little too dark, so Susan drew up plans for a glass extension, two storeys high, which added considerable extra space and light. Glass met 1890s brick. Once the extension was completed the garden was redesigned and the driveway repositioned. Susan and Gavin used a small gardening business that had put a leaflet through their door. Gavin felt happy to be giving the job to people from the local area.

See that? said Colin, indicating the glass extension, I wouldn't have that if you paid me. It's got no style. No style at all.

Does look quite shit, the youngest one, Bucky, said.

Ernie looked at it for a while in cool judgment, tilting his head this way and that. Bloody stupid, he said.

The woman appeared with tea for them in funny-shaped mugs. They all watched her as she took the tray back into the house.

Bit of an oldie, but kinda classy, said Bucky.

I'd rather have sleazy, said Ernie.

Everybody'd rather have sleazy, said Colin.

When it got to lunch the woman's husband brought them out various sandwiches. Was the woman a bit of a ballbreaker, they wondered, because there was the man making the sandwiches. We don't know that for sure, Bucky said, because she might have made them and just said to him, bring those out would you?

Exactly, said the thin one. You said she just said to him, bring those out would you? But don't be slagging the ballbreakers now. They can be alright. Miss Whiplash, those sort of ones.

In the house, Susan and Gavin worked in separate rooms on different floors. Gavin found being overly concerned with productivity counterproductive: it was better to allow disparate ideas, drawn from what he had thought and observed, and augmented by various things he had read, to coalesce in their own good time and in their own way. Sure, he had work to keep him going, consultancy whatnot. But they all knew him, they knew the way he worked. You couldn't force the kind of thing that he did. If sitting in the new house all the time had little to recommend it then it was fortunate that in the streets nearby Gavin could look in the windows of bakeries and second hand shops. He went to the same old cafe where he always left a generous tip. They always looked pleased to see him. Just the usual? they would ask and he liked that. Him, your man there and his funny wee leather bag. Back again. Funny wee jacket he wears too. Although she mostly didn't recognise him, he sometimes took his mother out on a trip from the nursing home. He put her in the front seat with a rug over her knees and they would drive off for an ice cream. On some visits he had driven down to the seafront but it had been bleak, sitting there licking the ice creams in silence and watching the waves roll faithfully, so now they stayed in the shop car park where at least there was some activity. He always had tissues in the car for when the ice cream ran down her face.

At the grand opening, the people's centre was gleaming and pristine. There were elaborate flower arrangements in the foyer and people flew over from London. It was said that the building was in line for several architectural awards, and certain to win at least one of them. A beautiful building that wouldn't be out of place in Chicago or Berlin, its multiple functionality was praised. Health centre? office space? dance studio? exhibition space? It was all of these things. There was a huge automatic door, efficient and welcoming and light flooded in an affirming manner into the huge space of the ground floor. A few weeks after its opening, Gavin took himself down to the centre when he needed another break. It was only a fifteen minute stroll from the new house. In the grand atrium however there was now a huge black vending machine that dispensed cans of Coke, Sprite and Fanta, Snickers, Aero, Mars bars, roast chicken crisps and ready salted. Gavin got a Coke and a bag of ready salted. The man on the desk said hello and Gavin said that he was just having a quick look. Was that alright? Look away, said the man. In the health centre area there was a water dispenser which was dripping onto the floor. The enterprise area housed several new business start-ups and consisted of an open space segmented by Perspex sheeting. Gavin watched two girls listen earnestly to a young man in a green sweatshirt. In the new house there were days when on the threshold of Susan's room he would loiter with intent. Want a coffee? he'd ask. What? No. Just in the middle of something here. Maybe later. Across from the enterprise area there was a schedule of events for the week—slimming club, Somme Society, two birthday parties—written on a grid on a whiteboard. On the first floor the smell of burnt bacon heralded the cafe. There was tea, coffee, bacon soda or sausage soda, and a couple of greasy newspapers on a table. Gavin got a coffee and read about the antics of some celebrities he didn't know.

Gavin was taking a circuitous route home from his visit to the people's centre, up and down the streets that ran off the main, when he came across Bucky Cash sitting with lordly composure on the wall outside his house. After their garden had been landscaped, Gavin and Susan needed someone to maintain it and Bucky seemed as good a person as any. He came round to do the garden for an hour or so every other Friday afternoon.

Bucky! Gavin said. Didn't know you lived so close.

A young woman with a child on her hip came to the door.

Bucky, she said. I need you a minute.

Oh. She saw Gavin standing there. Sorry.

When she had gone back inside Bucky said, That's Emma and Carl.

Right.

Emma shouted, Bucky would you come here a minute cos I need you to do something in the house.

Bucky made a face as though his work on earth was never done.

See you later on in the week then, Gavin said.

I'll be round the usual time, Bucky said.

As he headed back to the house, Gavin thought about Bucky's set-up. His girl was good looking enough with that top showing a good inch of dirty bra and those tight panty lines through the thin leggings. But that wasn't it. He didn't really care about that too much, even though with Susan it was all about those dreary and micro-managed handjobs. It was that Bucky had a child, Bucky was a father. From 1992 to 1998 Gavin had been too. But his daughter had died. He didn't want to think about her hair or the way she ran or her voice or the things she said although he did sometimes think about her funeral. He had hated it, because, and he was getting angry again just thinking about it, thinking about it as he was going back to the new house, because, if there was ever a time for nuance and minimalism it was not at the funeral of a six year old, for fuck's sake. What about pink feathers, the hair clips with plaited ribbons, plastic horses with multicoloured tails, those shops with the tat, their shelves emptied out over the seats, sprinkled down the aisles, thrown on top of the pavements? What about an exploding glitter bomb? Blasting out inane bubblegum pop, stupid shrill songs? But Susan had been in charge so it was all so unspeakably quiet and modest. I'm dealing with it. I'm getting it sorted. Please, Gavin, just let me do it.

Later that evening he told Susan that he had been to the centre.

Yes?

Yes, he replied.

All you could smell was burnt bacon, he said.

Well Gavin, I only designed it. I'm not responsible for what they cook in the cafe.

It's starting to look a bit shabby around the edges already, he said. Scuffed.

Susan frowned slightly. Always going to happen. With that volume of users. Inevitable.

Weren't that many people around when I was there.

Depends on what time. It's going to vary, said Susan.

I'll try going at another time then, said Gavin. Do a comparative analysis with the previous time I went. Yeah. Chart it in a graph.

But that would be the kind of activity anathema to Gavin. All those empty days, expanses of time when he did nothing, how could he bear them? She rarely turned down work, particularly if it was going to be taxing. She had hoped that she would have a breakdown; it would have been a relief. But it never happened. There was one time when she had stepped out in front of a car but it had missed her. Time wound down as it approached and she could see the dangling air freshener and the man's brown hair and it was like the start of an orgasm, but then he swerved and there was nothing. Everything continued oblivious. Susan wasn't a showboater: there was no hacking away at herself, no not quite overdoses.

Well, Gavin, that would give you something to do, wouldn't it? she said. It would help you occupy your time.

I have a life.

Oh so that's what it's called, she said.

It was the end of another week so Bucky was there. From the vista of the sitting room Gavin stood watching him load the cuttings from the hedges into black bin bags and empty the grass from the lawnmower into the compost pile. He was putting everything back in the garage when Gavin brought him out a beer.

Just call it a day, he said. Just take a seat and leave it— that's enough.

Place is looking pretty okay. Bucky surveyed the garden as if it were his own.

Yes, said Gavin, you're certainly doing a good job. Very pleased with how it's all shaping up.

Yeah not too bad at all. What's your missus up to today? he asked.

Oh not too sure, said Gavin. What I mean is, I don't know exactly what she's up to but I do know that she'll be back later. Flight gets in this evening. Can't remember if I'm meant to pick her up or not. Don't think I am. But I could be wrong.

What is it that you do yourself?

Oh I work from home.

Doing what?

Sort of advertising.

You make TV adverts?

No, said Gavin. I just come up with some ideas.

Ideas? That's it?

More or less.

That's a good number you've got. Bucky took a swig of beer. I wouldn't mind doing it, but I don't know where I'd get any of these fuckin ideas.

I could probably do with finding a few more myself, Gavin said.

After another few beers, Bucky rolled a spliff and they smoked it. He was surprised when Gavin expertly got the next one together.

When the car dropped her off the house was dark, but it was unlike Gavin to have gone to bed so early. As she walked down the path she could hear slow, heavy reggae. Susan walked round to the back where Gavin was sitting with Bucky.

Hey you're back, Gavin said, and Bucky noticed he went inside to turn down the music, as if his ma had turned up.

Bucky smiled and raised his bottle. Alright, Mrs Marsh? You just off the plane?

Susan said that yes, she was.

Hey come on and sit down and get yourself a drink sure, said Bucky companionably. Airports are always knackering.

All go well? Gavin said.

Yes, all fine. She put down her bag. I couldn't remember. I thought maybe you were meant to pick me up?

Oh God was I? said Gavin. Well glad you were able to get a taxi.

Yes. There were plenty of taxis.

Bucky's been working very hard on the garden, Gavin said. You'll be able to see it better in the morning. Oh and by the way I've got us sorted with a cleaner. That'll be good, won't it? Having a cleaner? It's Emma. He drained his bottle of beer.

Emma?

Bucky's girlfriend. She'll be starting, well do you think next week would actually suit, Bucky? That enough notice? If not, the week after maybe?

Bucky had said the people were fools. No harm to them, he said, because they are actually pretty dead on as people like that go but they are seriously, seriously stupid. They didn't have a clue what to charge and they were running around giving out stuff. Bucky said that the woman was like something off *The Apprentice*, one of the quiet ones in the background that turn out to be planning something all along, the sort that gets to the final and you wouldn't have hardly noticed them the whole series. The woman was jetting round the place, flying all over the globe, but then she didn't even know how much to pay a gardener, didn't know how much to pay a cleaner, probably didn't know the price of a pint of milk. Bucky was getting more for that one job than five others put together. And what they were going to pay her for the cleaning job was brilliant. Gav had apparently said they didn't want to rip people off, but everybody needed to rip everybody else off at least a bit.

Was that not the point? Bucky called him Gav nowadays. Bucky had said to her not to even bother trying to get Carl minded when she was working there. No point. Just bring him along, he said. Your man won't care. Might be a bit more of an issue if your woman's there, but your man, no, it won't be a problem. Seriously, he said, don't worry about it.

Emma had worked as a cleaner before, hoovering up other people's whatnot, hair and skin and the like. You'd just wiped their thickened piss from under the toilet seat, she had observed, and there they were, clutching their purse, how much do I owe you, giving you their tatty little note and some change, like they were the duchess. Hard not to laugh. You'd have to think about something really boring like a potato so you didn't laugh. At Gavin and his wife's place there was an alarm system and Emma had to key in five digits. The first time she went there, she wondered what had happened to all of their stuff because at home they had more crammed into their front room than there was in this entire place. It was empty as a church. The huge fruit bowl had a tower of apples, really green and shiny. Emma dusted the fruit, and if any of the apples were not looking so good, she replaced them with others from the fridge, taking care that they went back in exactly the same position. There was great suck on their vacuum cleaner, though. Powerful. When you opened their hot press, there were stacks of towels, all the same colour, folded in rows. Back at home Emma and Bucky just shoved the towels any way into a cupboard. One time she had shouted to Bucky when she was drying Carl, bring me a towel would you and he had yanked out a Carlsberg towel. I'm not drying the baby with that, not a Carlsberg towel. You're just being a dick, he had said. It's still a towel. Carlsberg or not. The woman's clothes hung on wooden hangers. There was a nice clink as they hit off each other. Rows of grey trousers. Rows of grey jackets. She wouldn't even think about trying them on.

One day when he was going into the kitchen to get himself something, the man Gavin said, Doing a good job there. Just let me know if I'm in your road. She'd thought, it's your house pal. I'm the one in the road. He had asked her if she wanted a coffee. No you're alright, she had said. And then she had added, my wee fella's sleeping upstairs in your spare room, is that okay? He had said that was fine.

In the people's centre there was a small library, housed on the second floor. Pod chairs and geometric white plastic created a sci-fi aesthetic which made the books seem relics from ancient antiquity. All Gavin seemed to be able to find were cookery books and biographies, mainly sports related. They were to the left and to the right. He had to call the woman over. Christ, he said. All I'm wanting to find are a few children's books. She pointed over to the corner with the cushions.

It had been two months since Emma had started as the cleaner. What had begun to irk Gavin was the amount of time that little kid spent in front of the TV watching saccharine US animations. He sat straight-backed on the floor with the curtains closed, mesmerised by the stuff. It couldn't be good for language acquisition and development. And Emma there: don't do that. Gonna kill you if you do that again. He wondered about the kid's diet. He wasn't judgmental, he would happily eat a takeaway every night of the week, but children needed something better.

Every week the kid arrived at the house eating a packet of Wotsits. Emma would quickly take them from him before they came in, but Gavin had seen. She sometimes gave him another bag when they were leaving. He had seen that too.

The next time they were there, Gavin was in the sitting room. Look what I found! he said to Carl, showing the books. You want to have a story? Emma needn't worry; he would keep an eye on Carl. It's no problem, he said. Seriously, no problem at all. Between the bouts of the hoover she could hear Gavin reading, putting on all of the voices.

Later that night, Emma and Bucky were having a drink after Carl had been put to bed.

What do you reckon to that Gav then? Emma said.

Oul Gav's alright.

You think so?

I do, he said.

Okay.

Why you asking? Bucky said.

It's just, oh nothing.

Nothing what? asked Bucky.

Nothing.

It's just, you don't think he's one of them paedos do you?

Nah, said Bucky. Gav? No way. Absolutely no fucking way.

He reconsidered. Well you never know, he said. Remember that fella—

Yeah, I know who you mean before you even say it, the guy that ran the old shop? Exactly Bucky. Who would've thought?

Why you think Gav's a paedo? he asked.

Dunno.

You just can't think it for nothing. Must be something.

Well, I'll tell you what it is, said Emma. It's just that he was sitting reading stories to Carl pretty much the whole time I was round there. And it was just the two of them in the big room. Kept an eye on it like. You know, I knew what was happening.

Right okay, Bucky said. Carry on.

No but that's it, said Emma. That's it.

Well, said Bucky after some consideration, I wouldn't be worrying. Thing is, look, what it is, he had a kid himself one time that died. Wee girl, died of one them things. Can't remember what it's called, one of them illnesses kids die of. Don't know what. He told me about it one night.

Oh Jesus, said Emma. She could see the little girl on a website, sad smiling photos, all the tributes underneath and the little candle emojis.

Yeah, well. Tough like.

What was the wee girl called?

Think it was Orla, Bucky said. One of those sort of names.

Aw that's nice, said Emma. Orla. Poor wee girl.

God love him, Emma said, he'd even gone and got a load of books from the library for him and everything. God help the poor fella.

Well, there you go, said Bucky.

So, hold on a minute. That means that your woman had a kid?

Yeah.

Fuck's sake!

The rooms in the new house were high-ceilinged with rococo cornicing. Although the grates were empty, most of the rooms had ornate fireplaces. An old house, it creaked. As Susan lay awake at night, she heard the floorboards relax to a restful position. The room where she worked was painted white and she could walk its perimeter in thirty-seven steps. The view from the window was of the path straight down below, although it was partially broken by a large, thick-leaved bush. That bush. It was aggravating, where it was. It would be impossible to avoid that bush and it was the only window. She needed to get a new laptop because working on the plane required something smaller than her present model. Deadlines in the diary, all underlined.

She didn't need Emma to come in here because she could clean it herself. If the child was there, she wouldn't come downstairs. One day she'd discovered it sleeping in the spare room. It was lying on its back in the middle of the bed, head turned to the side. Why did it live and her own child die? She hated the curve of its cheek and its socks, one of them half off, the slow rise and fall of its chest. She sat down on the bed beside it and laid a hand on its ankle. It felt warm. Its cheeks puffed a little as it breathed out and on its lips there were flecks of something orange that it had eaten. It would thrive, this child. It would make its sturdy progress. It would love and hate and grow old.

Emma was standing at the door.

I thought I heard a noise, Susan said.

Right.

And they both looked at the sleeping child.

Is that you nearly finished, Emma? Susan said, standing up.

I still need to hoover downstairs.

Well, I better not keep you back.

Susan closed the door quietly behind her.

*

When Emma had told Bucky she was pregnant, when she'd waved that little stick around, he wasn't unhappy. It was just one of those things. She wasn't the best, but she wasn't the worst. They'd got a place together and it was fine, although not as good as being at his ma's house. Things were better washed and better cooked there. It was a bit disappointing he had to admit to have to narrow everything down to one woman. He always liked attention. Manual job like his meant he was always in decent shape. Sometimes he caught the women gawping out at him. Objectify away, love, objectify, on you go. Especially if you're good looking. Not the old grannies, Jesus, yuck, but a couple of bored lonely housewives getting their gardens done, one or two of them of whom were reasonably hot? Most of the time it wasn't sunny enough to have the top off but it didn't deter him. He'd throw his head back, glug his can of coke slowly. Gav's wife though: one time he had seen her dark head in the kitchen and then later on up in one of the back rooms. He couldn't think that she wasn't watching him. Gav could do with losing some weight, that wadge of fat sitting on top of his belt. Bucky had started messing about with the hose, holding it in various poses, and then, accidentally on purpose had squirted it all over himself, a bit male stripper. He came into the kitchen dripping wet, beads of water on a hard tanned chest.

Towel, Susan said, holding it out with one hand while continuing to work at the table.

Thanks, Bucky said. He made a bit of an attempt to caress himself with the check tea towel but she didn't see.

Hose malfunction, said Susan.

*

A woman was at the backwash, getting her scalp bleach rinsed off. It was proving stubborn and the water kept running cold. It was Emma who was doing the rinsing. She still worked for Gav and Susan during the week, but she'd started doing one evening and a Saturday at the hairdresser's. She occasionally said to the woman to move her head back a bit, but most of her chat was with the girl beside her who was working up spectacular suds. So the woman says to me, Emma said, the woman I work for, she says, is cleaning what you want to do your whole life? Well no, I says, I got a childcare qualification. Oh, she says, is that so? Maybe Gavin should try to get that qualification too. He's got enough experience. I thought why you getting at me, cos, you know, she was slagging me because Gavin her husband sometimes looks after my kid when I go round. Nobody asks him to. He just does.

So what you say?

He'll need to wait till September if he wants to do NVQ level 2. That's when the enrolment is. She shut up then. But thing is she got me thinking what do I want to do and that's why I'm here. Excuse me love but could you keep your head back? Yeah, that's better. I could just see me owning my own salon eventually. Everything really like, mauve and gold.

What's her hair like, your woman that was doing all the slabbering?

Just, just kinda boring. Wee sort of crap bob. She doesn't really bother much.

The scalp bleach had dried out too much. It was hard to get it to shift. Emma rolled her eyes at the girl who had finishing rinsing away the suds. Why couldn't your woman keep her fucking head back?

*

The basalt cladding of the town's biggest gallery was already coming loose; the building was covered in thick net and strong hoarding to protect those passing from falling stones. A lump of basalt could kill. As she and Gavin went in, Susan looked to the top of the building where it met the sky. Every time they came to this place on a Saturday, their morning for going into town, Gavin made the same comment. Jeez, what a mess. Who designed this? Falling apart at the seams. It wasn't to do with the architects, Susan pointed out, it was the nature of the stone that had been sourced.

Yeah right, said Gavin.

Gavin's head was sore and he had made plans to visit his mother in the afternoon. Bucky had been round yesterday and after he'd finished it had been the usual, except that a friend of Bucky's ended up there too. This friend had a lot of good grass with him and they had smoked late into the night. Gavin woke on the sofa in the morning. Bucky's friend was an interesting guy who certainly had a lot of stories to tell. He seemed to know some very interesting people. Sitting outside as the sun went down a glorious pink, listening to music, smoking, it all felt real. And very, very cool.

Rock hard jet of total nonsense, said Gavin. Total bullshit. Do you not think Susan? What you're reading on the wall there. Steady rock hard stream of rubbish.

Meaningless conceptualising from a fucking collective, a dopey bunch of practitioner ponces. That's why the place was empty apart from Susan and him. He had noticed though, that on the floor below, there was a kids' section, where the paintings they had done were clipped with pegs to a washing line strung from one wall to the other. He wondered if he should bring Carl here. Bit far maybe.

There's art classes at the people's centre, you know, said Gavin.

Yeah? said Susan.

Oh yes, said Gavin. Very varied programme of stuff. There's mindfulness classes on all the time. Slimming clubs. A lot of very, very fat people around. Sometimes the kids use the big meeting space to play football. Saw it the other day when I called in. Well, I say football, it was actually a cushion they were using. Having fun anyway. Having a laugh. From your dim and distant past, do you recall that?

I recall, said Susan, that you used to be less of a prick.

Oh wow, how spirited, Gavin said. Bravo.

He'd been floating on wads of cloud but it was just the duvet over his face. Now awake Bucky lay there waiting for Carl noises, Carl movements but there was only the TV going downstairs. Half ten though: he needed to get up. Emma had left over an hour ago. But no matches, no chip pan fires, no swigging the caustic soda, wee Carl was happy enough watching his programmes. Today he was meant to go to Lurgan with Dale. He didn't feel like it, didn't really want to, but he would get some cash for going and all he needed to do was sit in the car. He'd be back before Emma but he didn't really want to bring Carl. He would grab something to eat and see if his ma was in. Last night had been alright but Bucky wished he hadn't said to Dale to come along. So I just turned round and I says. Most of Dale's life seemed to have been spent just turning round. Dale had a gun. The week before he went with Dale and some of his crowd away up the coast to a big forest park, pine trees really tight and close. They were there to shoot a deer. In all that dark and all those trees Bucky never thought they'd find one but they did. Bucky could remember when the lights were shining on it and it knew it was going to die. They slung it in the boot afterwards and it didn't seem so very big at all. But even so, Dale would have had a hard-on when he shot it. No butchers or restaurants wanted it. Why would they? Dale coming in with that thing.

There was no answer at Bucky's mother's. She would be down the town by now, buying her Saturday stuff. He could always ring Dale and say look mate, it just doesn't really suit, but he didn't really want to do that. It wasn't out of the question to take Carl with him, although he doubted Dale would have a car seat. He could always try Gav, he supposed.

It was Susan who answered the door.

Hi ya, Bucky said. Don't suppose I left my wallet here last night? Can't seem to find it.

Come in and have a look, she said.

Gav was just taking off his coat in the kitchen. Hey! he said. How's it going? You just caught us. We're just back from the town. You want a cup of tea? How you doing wee man? Carl was waving at him from the buggy.

No mate, no. You're alright. I'm just looking for my wallet. Didn't leave it here?

Not seen it.

Maybe it's in the house then. I'll need to have another search before I take a spin down to Lurgan.

Oh right. Lurgan.

Yeah. Bucky sighed. Better shoot to be honest. Having to bring this wee guy with me though. Emma's working at the hairdressers. Hope he's not going to get carsick. Right old journey that. Nothing else for it though is there wee lad?

Well, said Gavin, we're not doing anything. I'm not doing anything. Leave him here.

Does that mean you are going to cancel visiting your mother today? she said.

Bucky said, Aw no now. I couldn't do that. Couldn't leave him if you've got things on.

Well, Gavin said, doesn't need to be today. It's not set in stone. Could still go later anyway if I want.

You sure now? Only be an hour or so, two hours tops now, Bucky said as he left.

The child was lifted out of the buggy. It looked round the kitchen as Susan looked at the buggy, its folded plastic hood.

Why don't you take the child to see your mother? Susan asked.

Why would I do that?

She might enjoy seeing a child.

I doubt Carl would like it. It'd probably scare him. All those wizened faces. Place stinking of piss. Anyway, we're going to head out. You fancy a walk, Carl? Course you do. Where's that jacket?

Gavin had bought Carl a coat. No massive largesse, didn't want to embarrass anyone, it was just a plastic mac. There had been a couple of times when Carl had been at the house with nothing and it had been raining. He zipped it up carefully. They wouldn't take the pushchair. It was too annoying getting it in and out of shops. They would look at the waving lucky cat in the Chinese takeaway, go to the toy aisle in Wyse Byse, buy some streamers in the party shop, get an ice cream, have some lunch in the cafe.

*

The woman had parked her car to drop some clothes in at the charity shop and then she had gone to the bakery for an apple tart which she put on the passenger seat. As she was pulling out of her parking space she noticed a young child walking with his grandpa. They both had ice creams. As with all these things, it happened so quickly, the child saw something, maybe a balloon that floated away, or a funny looking dog on the other side of the road, and so he had broken free and dashed away. The child caused the woman to brake and down went the apple tart onto the floor. But the child scooted on into the road where he collided with a white van which sent him arcing into the air before he landed in the middle of the road. The woman in the car was the first to phone emergency services and the ambulance was there within minutes. A crowd gathered round, shocked and excited. Someone who had just bought a throw for their sofa pulled off the plastic wrap and placed the fake fur softly over the child. The howls of the man were what everyone said they'd remember. He sounded like an animal.

The paramedics needed information from Gavin about the little boy. When the police arrived, they did too. But, when he eventually could speak, all Gavin could say was that the boy was Carl. He didn't know his surname. If he had ever known it, he couldn't remember it. He was astounded that he didn't know it. Bucky, he said, was in Lurgan. But he didn't even know what Bucky's proper name was. He kept saying it, Bucky, Bucky, Bucky, as though the incantation would summon him. He didn't know Emma's other name either. He couldn't remember it ever having been said. He tried to phone Susan but he was shaking so much the policeman took the phone from him to find her number. The policeman spoke to Susan: had she a phone number for a man called Bucky? There had been an incident involving his son. Once the police phoned Bucky, they phoned Emma. But when the phone call came nobody could hear it with the noise of the salon, which was buzzing with the prospect of Saturday night. There was one missed call, then another missed call. So the police had to go round in a car. The one who came in to the salon was so handsome that half the women there thought he was a stripper. People turned to look. And then the boss called Emma over. She went out still wearing the latex gloves she had put on to apply some woman's tint.

When Emma arrived in Accident and Emergency, she saw Gavin. Where is he? What in the name of God happened? she screamed. Where's Bucky? What did you do? How could he just have run into the road? The veins in her neck stuck out. How? Why weren't you holding on to him? You couldn't have been holding on to him, you useless bastard, you—

She might have hit him had a nurse not come over and taken her by the arm. Just get him out of here because he's the one caused it. Get him out!

But he did not go. There was a row of chairs jammed in between a trolley and a folded up screen, and this was where Gavin took a seat. Wherever he looked, he saw the boy in the air. When he closed his eyes he saw it. He stared at his hand, turned it over, turned it back. Susan arrived and he began to describe what had happened, how they were on the road and Carl had just slipped away.

He just moved so quickly! One minute he was there and then next thing—

I know what happened. The police told me.

She sat down beside him. I do think he'll be alright though, she said. I do think that.

Bucky had been waiting in the car outside a house in Lurgan when he got the phone call. When they said it was the police, he thought at first it was some pals mucking around, but not when they said that there had been an incident involving his son. That conversation with Emma about Gav, oh Jesus what sort of incident? When they said a car accident he was almost relieved, but then Carl could die! He banged on the door of the house, shouted Dale! Dale!

Took him a while to answer. What's up?

The police!

Dale had looked around for them.

No, on the phone, Bucky said.

They're phoning us? said Dale.

Jesus no fuck's sake there's been a car accident with Carl.

They drove back at crazy speed and when he arrived they took him to the room where they had put Emma.

This is your fault, this is your fault! she shouted. You should've been looking after him! Why the fuck weren't you?

Oh Bucky, she said and started crying, long, shuddering sobs.

It was the first time that Gavin and Susan had both been in a hospital since their daughter died. They had each been there alone: Susan once cut her hand almost to the bone with a tin opener; Gavin broke his ankle. Susan sat next to the folded up screen and ran her hand along the faded material that over the years had sectioned off sleep and pain and all the rest. The room that Orla had been in and its perpetual twilight. Those last few hours, Orla had known that it was the end. Susan had seen it. That square room was the last thing that she would know. That chair beside the bed, wooden arm rests, green plastic seat. Was Gavin sitting beside her? She wouldn't remember where Gavin was? Was he even in the room? Of course he was. She couldn't recall him being there.

She only realised she was crying when she saw Gavin looking at her. He wanted to pull her to him, kiss her, but then a bright young doctor appeared. Mr and Mrs Marsh? The doctor told them that Carl had multiple fractures. Certainly he would be in hospital for some days, but he was going to be alright. His parents had been in to see him. Gavin had been in shock when he arrived; the doctor said he'd need a further examination before he left.

Susan went outside to wait for him. She leant on the rail and looked over the car park, saw the glow of the burger restaurant. There were some patients outside in dressing gowns and slippers and a few wheeled along their drips on trolleys. Most were on their phones. And then, because he was dying for a smoke, Bucky appeared. When he saw her he nodded over.

Looking alright for the wee man, he said. Thank Christ. But that sure is one of his nine lives gone.

Susan nodded. Such a relief to hear.

Yeah. Too right. See when I got that call, never going to forget it.

No.

Should see him lying up there, see the state of him. But he's going to live to see another day and that's the main thing.

I'm just waiting for Gavin, Susan said. He'll be down in a minute.

Bucky too leaned over the rails and looked out at the burger restaurant while he smoked the rest of his fag.

Better head back in, he said.

Sure. So glad he's okay.

The week after, Bucky called round to say that Carl was on the mend. He had a broken leg and a broken hip; he would have blurred vision for a while but he would be alright. Gavin gave him a bag of presents for Carl, sweets, DVDs and a few toys. Bucky shuffled from one foot to the other. He said that Emma wouldn't be able to clean for them anymore because she was having to spend more time with Carl now. He said that he would still do the garden if that suited, and it did, but he worked quietly and efficiently. He didn't have time to stop for a drink afterwards.

Susan undertook a major project involving the construction of a new shopping complex in Dubai. Over the following six months, it involved periods of time away. And after that she was more frequently required in the London office. The nights she spent in Belfast became fewer and fewer. Bucky and Emma split up. A week before Carl's fourth birthday, Emma moved in with Dale. The first time Bucky saw Dale with Carl, walking down the street, he thought he was going to die, it was ridiculous. But he found a great solicitor, a ferocious woman with a crew cut, who made sure he got reasonable access. Bucky ended up half in love with her. He kept on working with Ernie but Colin retired. Gav continued for a while in the new house, sitting in the glass box in the mornings, waiting for the day to turn right. But with Susan hardly ever there the place was too big for one person, and so they sold up and bought a flat in a new development down by the Lagan. On the rare occasion that Susan stayed there, Gavin fell asleep on the sofa. The neighbours complained when he played his music late into the night. In the nursing home, Gavin's mother refused to die.

The people's centre won third prize in an architectural award and featured in a national newspaper. Some teenagers and a doctor were interviewed about its functionality as a building and there was a profile of Thanasis, the architectural practice. There was a small photo of Susan. And then with no more ado the people's centre became part of the backdrop just like everything else, and in the untended patches at the back of the building, the knotweed grew towards the sun.

# Last Supper

The six-inch gash in the sofa's vinyl has been done with a blade, and whoever was responsible dug a hand into the foam to pull out a sizeable hunk as a souvenir. Now, no matter how carefully the sofa's taped up, it's going to look like it's been in the wars. Who was sitting at that spot today—table four, the low one, by the window? There were those young guys fresh out of the barber's who'd ended up wrestling with each other in a bout of laddish high spirits but unfair to judge because it could have been anybody.

Andy points it out to Jake.

I don't know anything about it, he says. I didn't see nothing.

Jake, I know that. I'm just saying, look what somebody's gone and done.

Rosaleen shakes her head.

The church is not sure whether to retain the coffee shop, which is run in collaboration with a mental health charity to provide a supportive workplace for those who need it. Good, but there are so many other worthy projects which could offer assistance to a greater number of people. This place loses too much money. Even members of the congregation, while considering the cafe as a generally worthwhile enterprise, tend not to frequent it. The older churchgoers prefer a little more ease and comfort, and the younger ones a venue near the church where in the evenings singer-songwriters, often pretty ones playing the keyboards or on occasion the ukulele, sing songs that could be about Jesus or their boyfriend.

The coffee shop is called Jesters. The pictures on the old menus were of a medieval jester, but when Andy got the new menus done, the graphics studio showed him a picture of a joker and asked if that would do instead. Sure, Andy had said, because it looked more or less the same. When the menus came back from the printers they featured the joker, but in addition the liberty had been taken of incorporating other playing cards into the design. Above sweet treats there was the queen of hearts and over breakfast there was the king of diamonds.

A member of the church who happened to call in was appalled. The new menus, he pointed out, were highly inappropriate: how could Andy have thought them acceptable when the Bible was so very, very against games of chance? Did Andy not know his Bible? Andy had said that it was just a menu, nobody was actually playing any card games in the place, but the church representative was adamant that the menus should not be used. To get them redone would have been both expensive and a hassle, so Andy had gone to Shop Kwik for a few black markers and made everyone colour in the offending images. Rebekah and Jake had messed about, swiping each other, tagging each other on the face with the pens. Rosaleen had coloured in with total precision. JD watched them do it. He said that the outlines, especially the joker and the jack now looked positively satanic. And he was right. The silhouettes did hold a slouching menace.

Andy has no doubt that the people he worked with over the years in other cafes and restaurants had their difficulties and problems too, but they just weren't made official in the way that they are in this place. In this place they keep it simple—soup, scones, toasties, baked potatoes, wraps, cakes—and no one is required to display culinary flair. When he first started, Andy saw that Rosaleen always went around with damp cuffs because she wore a sweatshirt under the Jesters polo shirt. Roll those sleeves up there Rosaleen would you? he had said. You're getting them soaking there. And when she had slowly rolled them up Andy realised, oh. Maybe roll them down again. Rebekah's polo shirt is tied in a big knot at the back so that it's stretched tight across her chest. It certainly improves the fit but it seems a bit unnecessary. Andy doesn't want to say anything about it though.

Come four o'clock it isn't likely that there will be too many more customers.

Can we turn off that racket now? JD asks.

It's Avicii, says Jake.

I'm not asking who it is. I'm asking can we turn it off?

It's young people's music, JD, says Rosaleen.

It's deaf people's music.

Oh don't worry about him, Jake, says Rosaleen. He's still stuck back in the eighties.

If only that was the case, says JD. If only.

Now don't you be going turning that off, Jake, says Rosaleen. Just you keep it on if you like it.

I might be stuck in the eighties, says JD, but with that haircut of yours, Rosaleen, you look like you were there at the birth of rock and roll. Oh look, it's Bill Haley with his Comets. Oh no, hold on, it's actually Rosaleen McCann.

I don't even like Avicii, says Jake. Turn it off if you want cos I don't care.

Andy calls Rebekah over to ask her to bring in the geraniums that sit outside in wooden boxes, and the tables and chairs for the smokers.

Me do it? Rebekah says. Seriously? I actually find those things really difficult to move, Andy.

Didn't realise they were that heavy, says Andy.

Oh they are, says Rebekah.

They're not, Rosaleen states.

Well they might not be for you, but they are for me.

That's because you can't be bothered making any kind of effort.

Not everybody's a big bloke like you, Rosaleen. Not everybody's a big bloke who can lug things around.

Not everybody's spoilt.

Ladies, ladies, please, Andy says.

JD has started wiping everything down. Give it another five minutes, Andy says, and then turn the sign around. Only tables five and six are still occupied and their people are bound to leave soon. Rosaleen takes in the geraniums, the tables and chairs, and also the Jesters sign. Keep a quick eye on things while I nip down the road would you, Rosaleen? Andy says. He wants to buy some tape and get that sofa sorted before the end of the day because things can fall apart so quickly.

Andy got the job at Jesters through the church. In those early days he was there almost every other night at one thing or another, discussions and seminars, workshops and praise nights. That was when he was still full of the newfangledness of it all. One evening at a meeting someone from the church had mentioned that they were looking for a person to work in their cafe in a supervisory capacity. Well he had nothing on at the moment. Would he be interested in doing something like that? Yes, but had he any experience? They needed someone who knew what they were doing. The upmarket Lebanese where Andy had been working, Byblos Nights, had just closed down. People in Belfast, it seemed, needed Byblos nights as much as people in Byblos needed Belfast nights. It wasn't long before he found himself sitting in the office of the charity, where he was required to have a short, informal interview.

On his way back to the cafe Andy sees the door open as a young guy and girl leave. They are both laughing and they stop to look through the window of the cafe before moving off up the road. And then out dashes Rebekah.

Hey! Andy shouts. Rebekah! What's up?

When he goes inside, Rosaleen is sitting at one of the tables with two women.

That, JD says, is a job for you.

What do you mean?

You'll see.

Andy, Rosaleen says, would you come here a minute because I think you need to speak to these ladies here.

JD winks. Good luck, he says.

One of the women is sipping a glass of water while the other looks on, solicitous. Well, the woman says, you come to a place like this and that's not a sight that you expect to see. You think a place like this is going to be one thing and it turns out to be something else.

You think, her friend says, you think that you're doing

your bit by coming to a place like this. Maybe you shouldn't but you do. It's not like there's not loads of other places on the road that you couldn't go to. Place is coming down with coffee shops.

Has there been a problem? Andy asks.

There's been a problem all right. People! She flutters her hand. People! It's not what I bargain on seeing when I go out to a cafe. And certainly not a religious place like this is meant to be. This is meant to be a religious place isn't it?

I'm sorry, I'm not getting this, Andy says.

Just as we're about to leave, she says, I thought I'll go to the toilet sure before we go and when I open the door what is it you think I see? Do you know what I see? Two people in your toilet.

They were having intercourse, her friend says. Do you know what I mean?

No, says Andy. Really? In there? He looks in the direction of the only toilet in the place: unisex, cramped, the tiny washbasin that gets hit by the door, the gooey soap and that toilet brush that still has the barcode on it. Logistically difficult enough, but maybe those two that he saw leaving managed it.

Are you sure? he asks.

Son, I'm sure, she says.

Her friend says, They're doing that and then they're touching stuff like the sausage rolls. You know, they're going out and working with the food.

Hold on, says Andy. You're not saying it was people working here?

That's exactly what I'm saying, she says.

Andy turns around to look at the counter where JD and Rosaleen are standing watching.

No, says the woman. Not them. That's not who I mean. The young ones.

They didn't even lock the door, says her friend. Imagine not even locking the door. You'd lock the door if you were even just going to the toilet.

They didn't even see me standing there, says the woman. They were both so involved in it.

This, it is clear, could make the papers: a solemn-faced photo of this woman with her hair just done, sitting in the safety of her living room, nursing a cup of tea that has been made in the non-sexual province of her own kitchen. And it would herald the end of the place.

This shouldn't have happened, Andy says. A shock, big time, for you and all I can say is that I am really sorry. He pauses. But what I am asking you, and this is me really asking you a big favour I know that, but could you just keep this to yourself? The people involved, they will be totally dealt with, trust me, this won't happen again, but could you just let this stay between ourselves?

Well… she says.

The people involved will be dealt with and they'll never do it again.

Well, I don't know, she says.

Please, says Andy.

Well I'd rather just forget what I saw, she says.

Sure it's not like the people working here are right in the head, her friend says. Wouldn't that be the case?

Well—Andy is about to contradict her, but he decides, no.

It's not the usual type of place, he concedes.

No, she says. Sure God help them.

He gives them both loyalty cards and stamps them seven

times. That means that next time our coffees are free! the friend points out. And he gives them the first slices of the new pavlova to take away. I just love getting the first slice, the friend says. Do you not just love getting the first slice?

When they're gone Andy finds Jake out the back of the cafe, smoking a cigarette. I can't believe this situation, says Andy. It's outrageous. It's a total disgrace. I mean, what were you thinking of?

Jake stares at the ground.

Could you not have waited till the end of the day? Would it have been beyond you to get a room somewhere? Could you even have done it out in the alley?

Sorry, says Jake.

That conversation I've just had to have with those two women, says Andy.

Sorry.

Well that's easy to say, isn't it? And you're only sorry because you got caught. I see your partner in crime didn't hang around too long.

He shrugs.

Well, I don't need to tell you that you'll be cleaning the toilet tonight.

He nods. Okay.

I hope you realise that this is actually a pretty big deal, Jake. It's not good.

I know, he says. You going to tell Ronnie and Michelle?

Andy had met Jake's foster parents once. Grinning faces in a dirty old estate car, three other kids and two dogs in the back.

Andy sighs.

No, I'm probably not going to tell Ronnie and Michelle.

They sanitise the surfaces. They steep the cups in the tannin solution. Andy rings off the till, Xs and Zs it, checks the takings with the balance and sets up a new float, puts the money in the safe. The takings, such as they are. He lodges the invoices and Jake cleans the toilet. JD mops the floor but he stops to lift up the duct tape Andy has left sitting on one of the tables. Here, he says, what do you wrap a hamster in, so that it doesn't explode when you shag it?

Dunno, says Rosaleen.

Duct tape.

How's that funny? says Rosaleen. It's just not funny.

Rosaleen had made potato salad a couple of days ago. There is a vat of it. She looks at the use until date.

This is going to have to go in the bin now, she says sadly. What a waste.

Sure give me a good few scoops of it and I'll take it home, JD says.

But it's off, Rosaleen says.

And you think the ones I live with will be noticing that?

JD shares, with an assortment of people, a once grand and elegant house on the other side of town, long subdivided into little cold rooms.

If you think they'll eat it, Rosaleen says.

Oh they will, says JD. I'll probably end up eating it myself.

Just don't like throwing stuff away, she says.

The religious experience which had brought Andy to the church and then the cafe had happened on the second night of his brother's stag. The first night had involved dry ice shots which had made him puke luminous bile. On the second, although she was meant to be the highlight, he hadn't enjoyed the stripper. Andy had seen her sitting in the bar earlier on, talking to somebody, sad line of a mouth, eating crisps. Later on, when she'd appeared in the back room, he could see in the white light the indentations on her legs where her socks had been. The whole place was clapping and whooping, but he had gone back to the hotel room with the tiny kettle and the UHT stix in an old ashtray.

He lay on the bed watching the telly for a while. Some of the buttons were missing on the remote. Andy had looked in the embossed folder of services available in the hotel and saw that someone had drawn a dick on the writing paper. Who was ever going to write a letter from this place anyway? Might do for a suicide note, he supposed. Someone had also drawn three swastikas in the bottom left hand corner. The folder said that the hotel had been a family concern for twenty-five years. Andy had looked in the bedside drawer and seen a tube of toothpaste and a sock with a few condoms stuffed inside it. Someone had been feeling optimistic about the trip. And there was a small Gideon's Bible that was even more plastic than the hotel menu of services. The paper was almost translucent and the print miniscule. He had to peer to see it. Rocky Raccoon, he thought. Andy opened a couple of random pages and tried to remember what happened to Rocky Raccoon, did he shoot somebody or did someone shoot him, and he didn't know if he'd been reading for two minutes or two hours because time seemed to stretch and bend and collapse and fleeting things that he had never been able to articulate before started to take form in a way more substantial than words. When he looked at the ceiling of the shabby room, the damp patch over in the corner and the crack around the lighting surround, and the repeated crescent stains where somebody had bounced a dirty ball on the ceiling the fragility of it all was overwhelming and the beauty too, because there was Marty's sweatshirt lying in illuminated folds like a sleeve from one of those old paintings, and there were the towels, brilliant white on the floor: centuries of people had cleaned away the dirt from sheets and towels, pummelling at the stains and the grime, rinsing it all away, the water circling down the drain, and endless lines of washing, high in the sky, billowing in a hard wind.

When everyone else has left and the cafe is silent, Andy gets out the admin folder with the various protocols relating to misconduct; it is clear that the correct thing to do is contact someone from the charity and someone from the church. But he closes the file and puts it back again. He stays late in the place. A couple of people think it's still open and try the door. Could they not have come during the day when they actually needed the business? We thought it was maybe BYO in the evening mate, they say.

There's been a few problems with the lights, the way they flicker at times and although he's no expert in electrics Andy stands on one of the tables to take a look. The place could look better. Before being Jesters it was Café Society, and before that it was Olive's. Olive, now an agent for industrial fridges, had once come in; she had expressed surprise that the décor was still the same. And I don't remember it being this small, she kept saying. They'd never met anyone from Café Society, but regularly there were debt collection letters from places in Bolton. Andy lifts everything out of the fridge to clean it and then moves on to the grill. The floor has already been mopped by JD, but Andy does it again. They got the five star sticker on the door when Environment Health came. Food Hygiene and Safety: Very Good. Structural Compliance: Good. Confidence in Management: High. He'd been very happy about it. Andy cuts the duct tape carefully and smoothes it on the sofa; in this light it is hard to discriminate between the black tape and the brown sofa but anyway, he moves a cushion on top of it. It'll hold up for a while. The man from the church had been right, he didn't know his Bible, he didn't know the names of all the books and the order they came in, he didn't know what happened in all of the stories, he didn't know what Jesus said next. But trying to be decent, that's it, and what more is there to say really? What more is there to know? Decent way of being. On the way home from the stag, Marty had asked him where he'd got to the night before. Big grumpy face on ye, nothing for it but to slip you a pill—but then didn't you just clear off? But Marty, he thought, had been only joking about that. He had been. He gives the coffee machine another polish.

Rosaleen is already waiting for him as usual in the morning, leaning against the shutters, the bread order and the containers of milk at her feet. Morning Andy, she says, blowing white air. Cold one, she says. Let's get that heat on quick, he says. Inside he turns on the lights, the dishwasher, the cooker and the oven, the grill and the hot plate, the bain-marie and the gantry lights. He checks the phone; there's a muffled message from Rebekah. She's not well and won't be in today. Then there's the hot water boiler, the coffee machine and the radio. Andy cleans the food probe again, files the dockets from the deliveries in the in tray. He puts the food hygiene sheets in the right place. Then JD arrives. Christ, it's cold out there, he says.

I've been freezing my balls off for twenty minutes waiting
for that bus.

Get a cup of tea sure, Andy says.

Rosaleen has started making the vegetable soup. Maybe
don't overdo the salt in that, Andy says.

Why, was it too salty the other day?

Well, I didn't really think so to be honest, Andy says. But
a couple of people did say they thought it was salty.

Sure, she says. I'll put no salt in at all.

No, put in salt but just not that much of it, says Andy.

Maybe what we should be using is sea salt, Rosaleen
says. It's meant to be a gentler taste.

Look, says JD. He's just saying to you, don't be putting in
so much of the fucking salt. That's all. Sea salt or whatever
kind of salt, don't put in so much of it. And don't be taking
things thick.

Jake arrives with the hood of his sweatshirt up.

Oh look who it is, the last of the red hot lovers, says JD. I
was just thinking last night, you know the way there's the
mile-high club, is there an equivalent for a coffee shop?

JD, says Andy. Enough.

Jake, when you're ready, he says, would you mix up the
scones this morning? All the stuff's already sitting out for
you.

Andy always buys a couple of papers to put in the rack,
but the workers only look at the front page so they don't get
messed up. Pointless, because even after the first couple of
people reading them there's buttery thumb smears in the
corners, pastry flakes in the folds. Sometimes people take
the papers with them, as a free gift. If anything was said
to them it would be, jeez, you've got your priorities right,
making all that fuss over a tatty old paper?

Rebekah decided not to turn up today? Rosaleen says. Her ladyship decided not to face the world today?

She's not well. She left a message.

Right, says Rosaleen. Not well. Sure.

Jake stares down at the bowl.

That's not going to mix itself, Rosaleen says.

Come on, son, JD says. So fucking what. There was a mate of mine, okay we're going back a few years here, but there was a mate of mine had sex in a concentration camp.

Well, says Rosaleen, I think that takes disrespect to a whole new level.

It does, says Andy.

Well what he said was, was that—wait a minute here, hold on till I get this right—was that it was an affirmation of life in a place of death.

Not very convincing, says Rosaleen.

No, says Andy.

Well, mate, says JD, don't worry about it, you had sex in a toilet in a cafe, not Belsen.

Well we'll need to talk about it later on, says Andy. It's not Belsen, but it is a workplace. What I need you to do after the scone mix is sort out that cutlery, that okay? And then I need you to go to the bank for a few coins.

Andy wonders about the effectiveness of the extractor fan. He'll have a look at it himself because getting somebody out is bound to be expensive. A couple of people come in for breakfast, regulars. The woman always wants a coffee with a jug of warm milk so that she can pour it in herself. Andy looks at the toilet door. There used to be a sign, for customers only, because people would come in off the street to use the toilet. But the sign kept falling off the door. You would say that it's for customers only, did you not see the sign, and they would say, what sign?—and then you would see it lying on the floor.

Mid-morning a man comes in wearing a suit and a shirt with the top button undone, no tie. He sits at the desk and gets out some plastic wallets and a laptop. When Andy goes over, the man greets him warmly. Andy! he says. How's it going?

Andy looks at his name badge which doesn't pin properly so it's always on the diagonal. Sometimes people do this: they see the name and use it repeatedly for a laugh. You have any red sauce there, Andy? Thanks, Andy. Wanna take that plate away, Andy? What time you close, Andy? Some people get a lot of fun out of doing that. JD refuses to wear the badge.

It's going fine, says Andy. How's it going with you?

You haven't forgotten, have you? the man says.

Forgotten what?

The six-month review?

Andy looks at the man and then what's on the desk. Looks at the heading on the paper that is sitting on the table, the heading in letters all friendly and small case. He's from the charity. How could he have forgotten about today? It's circled on the calendar in an orange loop. He can visualise it. The pen didn't work at first so there's a further orange scribble next to it.

Not sure we've met. I'm Aidan, he says. Good to meet you, fella.

He shakes his hand.

Andy says that that's right, he doesn't think they have met before. When it was Rosaleen's six-month review a woman came.

Yes, Aidan says. That would have been Carole. I'm her

line manager. I'm Deputy Head of Services.

Right okay, says Andy.

Aidan looks around the cafe. So I take it Rebekah's joining us?

No, says Andy. She phoned in sick this morning.

When?

First thing.

Right, he says. No biggie, Andy, but it would have been good if you'd let me know that. This is difficult to do without Rebekah actually here.

Maybe you want to come back another day?

No, Andy, it's fine. No hassle whatsoever, but I think we'd be better just working on through. Get down to business.

Sure, says Andy. Can I get you a coffee?

No thanks, mate, he says. I don't really do coffee.

Aidan opens the laptop and takes out a couple of documents from a wallet. Alright, he says, here we are. Rebekah. General impression?

Yeah.

General impression yeah?

Oh right. General impression, fine.

So, timekeeping for example, generally good?

Well yes, says Andy.

Attendance, today excepted obviously, generally good?

Fine, says Andy.

Alright.

Now here's when we're going to look at Rebekah's organisational abilities. How would you rate them?

Fine.

Higher order organisational abilities?

She's alright. It's not like she has to, you know, organise a lot of stuff here.

I see from the submitted data that we have here that Rebekah is actually very well qualified. Quite a few exams.

Right.

She'll be going on to bigger and better things eventually, says Aidan.

Suppose so, says Andy.

Now how is her social interaction with both the public and with other members of the team? says Aidan. Pretty good?

Andy glances at the toilet door. Fine, he says. She's alright. Everybody has their moments, in any workplace.

Meaning?

There's obviously a range of personalities here. Different people, different—

Sure, says Aidan. I maybe should have made it clear to you earlier on Andy, that in terms of this review, we are strictly interested in your perception, and our client's perception, although she's not actually here of course, of the satisfactory nature or otherwise of the working environment, for the client. Unless you are a clinician, which with the very greatest of respect I don't believe you are, unless you are a mental health practitioner it would be inappropriate for us to enter into that kind of discourse.

I've no desire to.

Just so we're clear on that, Andy.

We are.

Andy thinks of big flowers on a tired carpet bursting into bloom and running his hand over red plastic, poetry held in a damp stain on a ceiling.

Alright, Andy. So in general terms you've had no problems whatsoever with Rebekah?

There are thirty-eight bullet-pointed misdemeanours

listed under gross misconduct in the handbook but this misdemeanour is not there because no one thought to include it. It couldn't be downgraded to just major because major includes things like 'physical horseplay when working' and 'wilful wastage of time'.

No, Andy says, all going more or less fine. As you'd expect. Same goes for JD and Jake and Rosaleen.

In the absence of Rebekah then, Aidan says, that is us almost done. It normally takes longer because there should be a dialogue, involving the client. What we are aiming for is—he pauses—is a dialectic.

The other woman never got passionate and intense about a dialectic. The other woman, Andy remembers, wanted to know if there was somewhere on the road where you could get alterations done.

So do you want to reflect on the process?

What process?

The process that has just happened.

Andy looks around at Rosaleen down on her hands and knees scrubbing at a spot on the floor, and the menu propped up against the window with its coloured-in playing cards.

Not really, says Andy.

Well all that remains, Aidan says, is for you to sign this off. I need your signature just there, and then there. Just to verify everything. That's it. And sign that one too. Good.

And then he puts away the laptop and the papers. As he's going out he asks Andy, You ever been to Slim's Kitchen? No? Great place Slim's Kitchen. Andy watches Aidan head up the road until he cannot see him anymore.

Tutti! a woman shouts. Tutti Frutti! A large dog passes by, trailing its lead. Tutti Frutti! the woman shouts again, but the dog pays no heed. Andy attempts to catch the lead but it slips through his fingers. He follows the dog. It's always just a couple of feet in front of him until outside Shop Kwik it stops and begins gyring about, sending the lead flailing. A gang of young fellas now surround it, laughing. Get it! It's going mental! Get its lead, get it, here, I got it! but then the dog breaks loose again and the boys chase after it while the woman is still way down the road, calling its name in vain.

Andy goes into Shop Kwik. He sees the bank of sweets in front of him, the garden ornaments to one side, scales and sandwich makers to the left. There's the polyphonic sound of a row of animatronic fish, flexing as they sing. Somebody's gone down the aisle pressing all of the buttons. There's a spangled sign saying that raspberry cava (non-alcoholic) is on offer. He lifts a bottle. There's a range of cakes, discounted, that the label says have been baked in a country kitchen. He'll buy one, a Battenberg cake.

Jake has returned from the bank when Andy gets back to the cafe.

There was a queue, he says. Took ages.

Always does, says Andy. Everybody goes to that one because they closed the other two.

He probably called in somewhere for a drink on the way, didn't you? says JD. You ever had Spirytus, it's 95% proof.

Thought that was the name of a leisure centre, says Rosaleen. I finished off doing your scones by the way, Jake.

Did you? Okay.

So her ladyship's never graced us today, says Rosaleen. Wonder if she's feeling any better.

They are not busy at lunchtime. The food sits under the gantry lights crisping, drying out. JD goes around with the jug of coffee, asking people if they would like a top-up, a tea towel studiously draped over his arm. He's having a laugh. Rosaleen's soup remains mostly still in the pot. Some guys working on the site around the corner come in looking for a fry but they want to leave when they're told that the cafe doesn't do fries. There's soup, Rosaleen says. Would you like a bowl of soup?

They look at each other. Nah, not soup. You're alright. And off they go.

JD says when he was married that they used to have a roast chicken on a Sunday and then make soup with the carcass. It was always lovely.

You were married, JD? Didn't know that, says Andy.

Oh yes, he says quietly. A very long time ago.

Today it is Jake who brings in the flower boxes from outside and the tables and chairs which he stacks between the sofas by the window. He asks if it's alright if he leaves a bit earlier today because he's got a hospital appointment.

I told you about it last week, he says.

Oh yeah, so you did, Andy remembers. Well, you might as well head on then. We'll do the clean down.

Andy.

What?

Sorry.

Oh look forget it, Andy says. Doesn't matter.

Seriously, Andy says, never worry. But anyway, Jake, you know you won't be working here forever?

Jake shrugs.

Can you not think of something else you might want to do?

Dunno, he says. Can't really think of anything else right now.

Oh well, says Andy. I'm sure there's a lot out there.

Like what?

I don't know.

But anyway, he says, head on or you'll be late for that appointment.

They turn the sign around. They sanitise the surfaces again. They steep the cups in the tannin solution. Andy rings off the till, Xs it and Zs it, checks the takings with the balance and sets up a new float, puts the money in the safe. The takings, such as they are. He lodges the invoices while JD mops the floor. JD does a soft shoe shuffle with his dance partner mop as he croons some tune. Oh, for God's sake, shut up would you? says Rosaleen. She's checking the temperatures of the fridge and freezer, the chill cabinet, noting them down.

They're doing the final tidy when JD says that he's got something he wants to show to Andy. Check this, he says, and I don't think I'm wrong when I say you are not going to like it. Here, come over here, don't be letting Rosaleen see this. He has set down his phone and on the screen is the Jesters Cafe page. There is a one star review by Malcolm McCourt, who has a profile pic of a woman on a bike in a bikini.

Oh so what, says Andy. People have given us bad reviews before. Doesn't matter.

No, read it, says JD.

Oh, alright. And Andy takes it.

> If u know wats good for u don't come to this place unless you like your food cooked by a fat lezzer and an alkie. But, more importantly if u do not mind fucking in the bogs no mate I am not joking happened just now and we were there, welcome to da freakzone.

That'll get removed, says Andy. I'm going to report it.

But it has been shared six times already. Someone has offered the comment, OMG, ha ha.

Andy looks around the cafe, coffee machine still shining.

Well, they should get their facts right, says JD. I haven't really been an alkie since 2009.

Nobody'll pay any heed, says Andy. But there is every chance that the church will find out about this. It will be the excuse they need. They'll see where he signed Aidan's sheet to say that the girl who had sex in the toilet is a good worker in all respects.

What are you fellas talking about? Rosaleen asks.

Oh nothing, Andy says. I'm just saying, come on and sit down for a minute or two, that's all.

He gets out the non-alcoholic cava and the Battenberg cake, puts them in the middle of the table.

Just thought, he says. Might as well, it's the end of the day sure.

Yes, says Rosaleen. Her hand is up the sleeve of her sweatshirt. Yes, come on and sit down JD. Take yourself a seat.

But I'll tell you what, do you not think we can do better than this? I think we can, says Rosaleen. She goes through to the back and brings out a tablecloth—only paper but white—and lays it over the long table, smoothes it down.

Do we have wine glasses? she says. I don't think we do now.

Sure use those other ones, says JD, the ones for the ice-cream sundaes. When we used to do the ice-cream sundaes. Those shrinky dink glasses.

They sit around the table, Rosaleen, JD and Andy.

Andy cuts the cake, reveals the pink and yellow motley of the Battenberg, and they all take a slice.

Bit dry, says JD. If it wasn't for the marzipan, you'd think you were eating bread.

It's alright. It's not that bad, Rosaleen says.

Andy takes a bite. Put it this way, he says, I can see why it was on offer.

See that joke I told you the other day, says JD, I got it wrong. You remember that joke? Yeah? I said the punchline was duct tape. But it should have been why do you wrap—why do you wrap a hamster in duct tape? Answer: so it doesn't explode when you—

Yes, JD, alright, says Rosaleen. I think we can work it out. Don't think it's any funnier that way around.

Outside the light is starting to wane. It was cold this morning but it will be even more pitiless now.

Look, says Andy, still a bit left in this bottle. And he shares the dregs between the three sundae glasses, which they clink.

# Arab States: Mind and Narrative

A handful of bills and a takeaway menu on the mat, a solitary black banana in the bowl, but no Jimmy. Paula returned early from her holiday and he wasn't there. By lunch the next day he still hasn't appeared. He's left his phone by the bed so Paula rings Scott.

Dunno, he says. But you think he'll be back for the 23rd alright? We got that snooker thing happening with my brother-in-law.

Well, I don't know about that, Scott, because I don't know where he is, and because I don't know where he is, that's why I'm ringing you.

Jimmy broken at the foot of a cliff as the faithful waves keep on rolling, Jimmy face down in a black puddle in an alleyway. The crazy burst of glass as he's propelled through the windscreen, garage carnations sellotaped around the pole for the roadside memorial. Ellie doesn't know where he is either.

Mum, Ellie says, you're heading off sometime soon, aren't you?

No, I'm not. Because, know what, I'm back.

Oh. Right.

A woman in work called Anne walked into the sea, leaving her good coat and shoes neatly beside her handbag on the sand. On a work night out Paula sat next to her and explained why the new rota for the fortnight was so unfair. She produced a calculator at one point to illustrate the minutiae of the injustice. Anne smiled and seemed to understand. When Dr Donnelly brought them together to tell them the terrible news, Paula thought of the calculator.

Well sure you weren't to know, Jimmy said.

Well I know that! I know I wasn't to know. That's not the issue.

So what is the issue then?

Oh just leave it.

Paula gets a message from Ellie who has found out that Jimmy is at a blues festival in Strabane and will be back on Saturday. He's still in the land of the living. A blues festival in Strabane: he should have called or sent a message. He should have left a note. But Jimmy didn't know that she was going to return early, so had he written a note, it would have been a note to nobody. He did ring at the start of the holiday but they had just brought the desserts, which were quite spectacular. Phone you later, she said, but then later he was driving.

When Paula goes back to work the next day they are pleased to see her return early. There is a glitch in the system that she is able to sort out within ten minutes.

Your holiday good then, Paula? Amy asks.

Fine. But we came back early. My friend's mother wasn't well. Yeah, death's door at one point but then, once we'd rearranged to come home, an improvement.

You want your lunch from the sandwich place? I'm texting the order through now.

Sure. That usual thing of mine, the salad, but get me a Diet Coke today would you?

Okay, says Amy. Actually, Paula, that's not part of the deal. It's a filter coffee or a tea for, you know, the deal. We get four for three but if you're not getting coffee or tea then that means we don't count as the deal. Although, you know, get what you want, it's up to you. If you want a Coke.

Well it was a Diet Coke.

Diet Coke then.

So basically I need to drink a drink I don't want so that everybody else is part of the deal? That's what I have to do?

Oh don't be getting on like that, says Amy.

Just get me whatever then. Anything'll do.

There's a TV in the waiting area of the surgery. At lunchtime when the local news comes on, the final story is about the blues festival in Strabane. A guitarist is being interviewed. How you finding Strabane? he's asked. Better than Montreal, he says. We were at the Montreal blues festival last August. They didn't think guys from Warrenpoint could play the blues but when they heard us they woke up and smelt the coffee. There's footage of people milling around outside a large tent, the sound of a blues shuffle. When later a child is sick into the toy box the debate is whether to clean the individual toys or throw the whole stinking box in the bin. They spray the plastic toys with sanitiser but the pages of the books are translucent with vomit so they get chucked.

Paula sits in Jimmy's spot that evening, the leather chair with the good view of the screen. She takes one last flick through the channels to see if there is anything worth watching. Some dopey thing for half an hour is all she wants: have a last cup of tea and one of those biscuits. And then a face appears that she recognises, older and more tired looking, a little creased, but it is still him because there is the confirmation of his name at the bottom of the screen. Paula knew him as Ryan Hughes but it's Ryan Kedrov-Hughes who is now in front of her. He looks frustrated as if it's difficult to articulate the complexity of what he's just been asked. He ruffles his thinner hair and begins an answer full of qualification and proviso. Even though Paula doesn't know much about Beirut, she can tell it's a nuanced response. But then Ryan Hughes used to answer like that even if the question was, you wanting tea or coffee? His voice is almost but not quite English. You can still hear a slight Belfast stodge. Unlike the others in the studio he isn't wearing a tie. Style wasn't really one of Ryan Hughes's concerns back then because to be overly interested in clothes was really just a bit uncool. Commodity fetishism was uncool. Loads of people at university had been interested in politics, Paula included, but it was mostly local stuff. Ryan Hughes always seemed part of something bigger. When he was a teenager he'd attended a summer camp for the junior wing of the Socialist Unity Party of Germany.

No longer heading to bed, Paula goes to the computer where she has to close down Johnny Winter Live Copenhagen 1970, Rory Gallagher 'Bullfrog Blues' 1972, HotRoxMinx. As she searches for Ryan Kedrov-Hughes, things begin to come back, little details start to accumulate. His mother's family was Russian, she remembers, which explains the Kedrov. Kedrov-McCrea. Paula Kedrov-McCrea. His trajectory involves Reuters, university in the States, work for Al-Jazeera and some acronym she doesn't know. Another search: Ryan Kedrov-Hughes and partner.

Clicks images. There are just photos of him in studios, a few TV screenshots. But there's one with a woman, partially out of the frame. She's wearing a black coat, tightly belted, dark hair half over her face. Another zoom and the photo fragments.

I didn't know where you were, Paula says when Jimmy comes through the door the next day. I hadn't a clue. I thought something had happened to you.

Gimme a kiss, he says.

He produces two T-shirts from his holdall. North-West Blues Festival is printed across them.

But wait till you see this, says Jimmy, rolling up his sleeve to show what he's had done: a tattoo of a guitar, surrounded by roses. The ribbon running across the guitar bears the legend Born to Die.

What do you think?

What do I think? says Paula.

Yeah, you like it?

States the obvious.

The other T-shirt's for Ellie, he says.

Paula wonders if it will fit her. She and her girlfriend Meg go to barbecue restaurants, rib shacks, where they consume amounts of food that would keep a family in the dustbowl going for a year.

States an indisputable fact, I suppose, says Paula as Jimmy rolls down his sleeve.

By the end of the week there's a stack of newspapers for Jimmy to use to light the fire. She's still shaky on areas like economics but is starting to feel more confident about Middle Eastern politics. She watches all the useful TV programmes, but because there is so much happening in

Ukraine at present, Ryan Kedrov-Hughes doesn't make another appearance.

Jesus, this stuff is so depressing, Jimmy says. This news never seems to be off the telly.

Yes, Jimmy. It's on every day. That's how news works. Things just keep on happening, day after day.

Killing, blowing people up, terrible, but not a lot you can do about it, just the way it is.

There was one time when a crowd of them had gone to an old man's bar after a lecture but over the course of the afternoon everyone drifted off, leaving the two of them together at the table. Paula could still remember that earlier Ryan had been talking about how the lecturer had made several errors regarding the Soviet Union's economy in the 1960s. Nobody cared much, but they listened anyway because it was Ryan Hughes. Ryan asked her if she would like to meet later on. He might have asked if she was free for dinner. Back then, however, did anyone actually go for dinner? They didn't. She had said yes, but then remembered that she was meant to meet Jimmy that night. She'd only been going with Jimmy a few weeks. So she had said maybe some other time but not that night. Alright some other time then, he said, and what followed was a short silence. But then there was also that other time when during a tutorial he said, Good point. I think that Paula is spot on there. And also, not to be omitted, there was the occasion when he had been behind her in the queue when she was getting money out of the cash machine. It was raining and they had exchanged a few words under her umbrella. That's what she remembers right now, but that's not to say there weren't other times too.

Paula sends off for lots of books and they sit on the kitchen table.

What's all this about? asks Jimmy.

Paula shrugs. Just interested, she says.

Oh yeah? Well rather you than me. Look at that one. Must weigh a ton.

Nobody's asking you to read them, Jimmy.

You thinking of doing a course in all that?

Nope.

She lifts the books to take them through to the other room.

Maybe do a course in how to be slightly pleasant, Paula, he says. That on offer anywhere, do you know?

She's reading the book section of the Sunday paper when she sees that a crime writer's appearing at a book festival in Newcastle upon Tyne. In smaller letters, much smaller letters underneath, are those also appearing: this person, that person, never heard of him, never heard of him, never heard of her, and Ryan Kedrov-Hughes. He would be talking about his forthcoming book, *Arab States: Mind and Narrative*. There isn't a photo, just one of the crime guy sitting in front of a bookcase. Paula goes on the computer to order the book. While she's there, she has a quick look at flights to Newcastle, which are surprisingly reasonable.

By the way, Paula says one day when she and Jimmy are having their tea, I don't suppose you ever remember me talking about Ryan Hughes? We're going way back here, you know, university? We're going back years.

No.

You don't remember me ever mentioning him at all?

No. Never heard of the fella.

Are you sure? You sure you can't remember him?

No.

Well he's not called that anymore anyway, says Paula. He's called Ryan Kedrov-Hughes. Just thought you might remember him. He's on the TV these days. Politics shows.

Oh well now you've told me that he's on the politics shows I know exactly who you're talking about.

You do?

No.

Actually, hold on, he says, that fella, I think I do actually know who you mean.

Yeah?

Yeah. He was always at Mick's Christmas parties. Mick was the only person from your course that was normal. Mick was dead on. That guy you're on about was always there. Always in the kitchen crapping on about something or other. You know, turn the music down so that I can talk because people really need to hear what I have to say. Think I actually mighta had a run-in with him once. Sorta Lord Snooty type. Lord Snooty type of fella.

Might not be the same person, says Paula. He wasn't like that at all. Ryan Hughes was actually incredibly left wing.

Well this guy I'm thinking of was a bit of a dick, says Jimmy.

Well the guy I'm thinking of wasn't a dick, says Paula.

Might not even be the same person. Did you know him well, the person you say wasn't a dick?

No.

Well then he might have been the dick that I'm talking about.

He wasn't a dick, says Paula.

*

Paula sits at the table, the brown cardboard package in front of her. Jimmy has gone out for a drink. His parting words were, He was a dick by the way. With a little tug the serrated strip gives easily and Paula puts it to her face to sniff the new glue. The smell of cleverness. Hardback. *Arab States: Mind and Narrative.* The cover is a little austere, a blue which could be sea or sky. Ryan Kedrov-Hughes is in a bold, block typeface. On the back there's a small picture of him, high contrast black and white. It's reasonably flattering. Chapter One is preceded by three or four pages of maps, a bit daunting maybe, but a book like this is obviously going to make demands on you. Demanding and rewarding. It's not really for the casual reader anyway.

She turns to the acknowledgements at the front. Yes, yes, yes, all the usual people are there, my editor, my colleague at here, my colleague at there, patience, forbearance, uh huh, uh huh, and then Sabina Kedrov, that must be his mother, that's okay, and then it's thanks to Fazia, for the breakfasts. Fazia for the breakfasts? That seems a bit trivial. Paula thinks of a taut woman cooking a breakfast wearing only a man's white shirt. Assembling a breakfast, no splats of fat on that white shirt. Still, still. Breakfasts can be bought down any street. Fazia probably works somewhere he goes to, used to go to for his breakfast. He's there with his laptop making a few notes, answering a few emails. Fazia's an old lady who works in a Turkish cafe somewhere. So cool of Ryan Kedrov-Hughes to acknowledge in his book an old worker who prepared his meals.

Paula starts going to the cinema, mostly the one at the university. She sees a film set in Jerusalem about an orthodox butcher who falls in love with another man. It doesn't end well and Paula finds herself crying a little. The discussion afterwards, chaired by a lecturer in international studies, is on the theme of 'The Multiple Meanings of Urban Citizenship and Identities'. The woman next to Paula has a few comments to make on secular identity. After the final round of applause, Paula asks her if she has ever been to Jerusalem.

No, the woman says. Not in a long time.

Although she has lived in Belfast for many years now she did travel extensively when younger. She asks Paula if she has been to Jerusalem.

No, says Paula. But I've a friend who's spent time there.

I see.

Yeah. You may well have heard of him. My friend. Ryan Kedrov-Hughes. He's on the TV sometimes.

I'm terribly sorry but I haven't, says the woman.

No? Paula says. Well I would thoroughly recommend his book, *Arab States: Mind and Narrative*. I'm two thirds of the way through it.

Yes, Ryan Kedrov-Hughes, says Paula.

She checks the email one more time and thinks again that the tone's fine. But she still hovers over the send button. She is messaging to say that she will be attending the event on Friday in Newcastle upon Tyne. It's a generic work address rather than a personal one, but it was all she could find online. It's hard to know quite how to sign it off. She had tried at first *your friend of yesteryear, Paula*, but that sounded too twee and whimsical so she changed it to Paula McCrea (Pearson) QUB 88–91, which couldn't be faulted on fact.

So exciting next day when an email comes back.

Paula: good to hear that you'll be able to make it along
to the event at Gosforth Library.

Best, Ryan.

Under the message there are links to two sites where the
book is now available for purchase. It feels a little generic.
No harm in making things a little less oblique at her end.
She composes another one.

Yes: coming over from Belfast specially!

Slightly more effusive, but then that, Paula thinks, is the
point. No further email comes from Ryan Kedrov-Hughes,
but then he is probably 'on the road' by now.


She finishes work at lunchtime on the Friday and Ellie
picks her up to take her to the airport.

Yeah, says Paula. Just one of those shopping trips, saw
it in the paper.

I know, Dad told me.

So cheap, couldn't believe it. That big shopping centre at
Gateshead, there's everything there.

Yeah. Dad said. Well, rather you than me.

Which is why I'm going and you're not.

True, Ellie replies.

Maybe you and Dad can come around for something to
eat on Sunday, she says. We want to chat over something.

Sure, says Paula. Why not? That would be nice. They
have stopped at the lights. When it was raining and she
was getting the cash out, the colours were so intense. Rain
on a dull day makes everyone's eyes so clear.

So what do you think? says Ellie.

About what?

About what I've just said. About me and Meg getting a
civil partnership.

149

Yes, sure, says Paula. Seems like a good idea. Why not?

Seems like a good idea? Well, okay, Mum, know what, you're right: it is a good idea.

That's good then, says Paula.

The plane is delayed but that allows her to have a couple of pre-flight drinks. She feels enigmatic, perched on a stool, drinking alone in the dimly lit bar area, looking slightly, who's that guy, slightly Hopperesque. She takes out her book and realises that instead of lifting Ryan's she's brought a different one, *Translating Dissent*, which also has a blue cover. That's very unfortunate but at the same time it's an indicator of the range of her reading. She looks at a couple of pages, then puts it away again in favour of the drinks menu and its narrative of whiskey production in Ireland. The flight gets delayed again. Fog somewhere, apparently, holding everything up. Amazing that Jimmy could remember Ryan from Mick's parties because she can't.

On the plane she gets the window seat. When the flight attendant comes along the man with faded red hair sitting next to her orders a double gin and tonic. He says he needs it. He's going over to a funeral of an old friend.

I hate graveyards, he says. Although I find myself in them increasingly.

Paula says to the flight attendant to make that a gin and tonic for her as well, although not a double.

There is an announcement about special offers on board that include underwater watches, chocolate and various beauty products, all costing substantially less than on the high street and only available for a limited period. Paula takes the inflight magazine to read more about the illuminating cream that has been brought to her attention.

It seems very good and it's not often that she treats herself to something like that. The flight attendant takes her credit card payment and the cream in its silver box is hers.

Good luck with that, the man with the faded red hair says.

Paula takes the Metro to the hotel which it says on the website is under independent ownership. It had been a toss-up between this hotel and a budget chain in the centre, but this one is nearer the venue for the book event. The blue carpet is stained and from the window she sees two bags of cement in a wheelbarrow down in the yard below. Paula didn't even know you could still get candlewick bedspreads. Imagine bringing someone back here. Ryan Kedrov-Hughes is probably staying in a swish five star, but she hadn't even clicked on the four star tab. Although he might well appreciate the frugality of this place, conspicuous consumption not being his thing. It's great that there's a minibar, something else that you don't often see nowadays. She reaches for one of the cute little bottles of wine and opens a packet of nuts. Decline of the minibar: discuss.

Paula needs to get ready. It's important to consider where best to sit at this thing. The front row is out for a start. Way too conspicuous. The front row might be reserved anyway for VIPs or people with disabilities. Depending on the size of the crowd, a good move might be to sit at the end of a row because that would ensure a degree of visibility. She should try to make a contribution or ask a question. Interesting perspective, Ryan Kedrov-Hughes might respond. Or he breaks off from what he is saying: Sorry, but I've just noticed a very old and very dear friend of mine in the audience. Cue slight wave, then slight return of wave.

All those recent internet searches never turned up whether or not Ryan Kedrov-Hughes has a partner. On balance, he probably has, a UN interpreter say, quick and slinky. The candlewick bedspread has a nice feel. But what does it even mean nowadays really to say I have a partner? There are various permutations, gradations. It's great to leave work and just jump on a plane. Dr Donnelly earns six times her pay but he can't grasp how to work the computer, she's shown him again and again, and then aren't those locums so jumped-up? Working there the rest of her days, she knows it. She looks at the open door of the minibar. Might as well look forward to the leaving do at the La Mon, and even then it won't be the restaurant, it'll be the lounge menu. One of the locums saw Paula's book beside the computer. The Middle East? Where's that then? she said. Somewhere in between Ballyhackamore and Cregagh Estate? The others had a laugh at that, Amy repeating it just in case anyone didn't hear it the first time. She would have looked humourless if she'd got annoyed.

You would rather do something else, Paula? You think you could have done something more? Who doesn't think that? Is there a single soul? What is it, exactly, you'd rather do, that you think you were really so cut out for? Dunno. Dunno do you? Shrapnel from the barrel bomb slices through the nine-year-old's soft arms so a big deal that someone feels they could do more than work down the health centre?

The room lurches to one side when she rises from the bed. She pulls her dress, last worn at Anne's funeral, out of her bag. Black and matte and severe looking possibly, but it's not a party. Severe is alright because no one would want to look laugh-a-minute at an event of this kind. She'll apply plenty of the illuminating cream. Nice smell, violets, like those sweets. Can you still get those sweets? The effect isn't too radical so she applies more, concentrating on the eye area. Paula can't believe how creased that new coat has got when it was folded so carefully. Perhaps she shouldn't wear it but no. She wants to wear the trench coat with the belt. Steam's what's required. It's an old trick. Creases just drop out with a bit of steam. In the bathroom Paula twists the shower dial around to the thick red line and sets it blasting, then turns on the bath taps, the sink taps. The coat she hangs from the shower rail. She can finish her drink and give it a few minutes to work.

Some other time then, Ryan Kedrov-Hughes said in the bar. And then there was silence. Nothing materialised, no funny story or pert little question. Maybe she looked at the configuration of ice in her drink, how it slowly moved, looked at a beermat. Said, probably time for me to be heading on. But then silence is articulate and what's not said is felt not heard. She could see that now.

There's knocking at the door. It's a man from reception to say about the water. She's running a lot of water. And, yes, she can hear the roar of the water and now the steam escaping from the room into the corridor. He says that it's the other residents, they're complaining because she is using all of the water. Would she please turn the taps off? And then he pushes past her into the room to turn off the taps. He says as he is going that they're only a small hotel, so really madam, either shower or bath, one or the other.

But most of the creases have gone, although at the back that kick pleat is sticking out at a ridiculous angle. Belt the coat tight and it's even worse. She's a sack of potatoes tied around with string. She throws her shoulders back and puts one foot forward, shoves her hands in the pockets. Now that is not so bad. Cold war spy: low-ranking. All that steam will have negated the effect of the illuminating cream so she dabs on some more.

At reception she asks about where she needs to go. Oh yes, Regent Centre. That's right. She remembers it once the woman says it. There's a big stapler sitting on the table behind the reception desk.

Could I borrow that a minute? Paula asks.

She takes off the coat and staples the pleat at the back so that it sits in place.

Thanks, she says.

The air outside is cool and she is surprised that it is dark. But of course it's dark. How could it not be dark? *Translating Dissent* weighs heavy in her bag. When she takes a seat on the train she lifts it out but with the movement the words are dancing on the page. The event will probably be starting soon, so maybe she should have left earlier. With the movement of the train and all those lines jumping and slipping she starts to feel sick, so she puts the book back in her bag. At least the journey won't take long. Where'll she go afterwards? Or where will *they* go afterwards? It could just be Ryan Kedrov-Hughes and her. No need to be presumptuous, but it is a possibility. There will be all sorts of places here, no doubt: members' clubs, after-hours clubs and that kind of thing, all sorts of people there, people you wouldn't have heard of, but plenty also who you *would*, like…

       like

            like

                  like

                        Jimmy Nail!

No, but who else? Come on. Wittgenstein lived in Newcastle at one point, she had been surprised to read that, Wittgenstein, but clearly he's not available at this juncture, and what would she say if he was? Best he's not really because what would she say? She tries to remember the points about Arab States that she could make, points on different things, subpoints, sub-subpoints, but nothing is staying in her head as things fly away around the carriage, up, down and out that one open window.

She comes out at Regent Centre to cubes of offices and a couple of illuminated logos and when she looks up there's the blue glow of a line of computer monitors that no one has switched off. And what is that over there? A motorway? A dual carriageway? It's starting to drizzle now so she turns up the collar of her coat, pulls the belt tighter. She never thought of bringing an umbrella and yet it would have made so much sense to bring an umbrella. Those boys on top of the bus shelter, they shout something, but is it to her or somebody else? She turns around but nobody's there, nothing but a streetlamp that thrums like a pylon. Something like that could possibly explode. Never mind Wittgenstein, why didn't she consider downloading a map? She could look at the Metro ticket to see what time it was a while ago when she got on the train but she doesn't know where the ticket has gone to. One good thing though, the creases are going to be well and truly out of the coat because they won't survive roaming around in the rain, but she would have thought there'd be a signpost somewhere. What's the name of the place anyway?

There's a building that seems to have people going in and out, and closer there's a sign that says Welcome. Doesn't seem like... seems an odd... but quick clicking steps take Paula to the door. Inside there's echoing blue and that smell, it's so familiar… she knows what it is but she can't quite place it. I'm here for the event, Paula says to the man and woman behind the glass who are wearing identical blue tops. Okay, the man says and then turns to the woman to say that this lady here is here for the event. Here for the event, what event? What event, love? the woman asks. And the man says, What's the event? It's the thing. The thing! The thing, you know the thing I'm talking about. Arab States! *Arab States: Mind and Narrative.* Arab States, the woman says. What's that? United Arab Emirates? Emirates Stadium? Is that what you mean? No, not a stadium, I'm not talking about a stadium, it's *Arab States* by Ryan Kedrov-Hughes. He's talking about his book and I'm meant to be there.

The woman's shaking her head, doing a big doleful face. Don't know. And the man's shouting over to somebody in a room out the back, anybody ever heard of what's his name, sweetheart? Ryan. Kedrov. Hughes. Dum de. Dum de. Dum. What it is, is chlorine, that's the smell, funny the way she didn't know and then all of a… whoosh… how could you possibly not have known? Whoosh… The smell never came out of the costumes or the towels and the spectators' gallery was all clammy echo. Ellie was all of a piece but the other kids they were sleek, they could dive. Nice to watch the other kids, how they glided through the water, she would rather have watched the other kids. Another man in blue comes along and he's saying that he's never heard of him, this Ryan guy. I don't reckon you're in the right place love, I don't reckon you're in the right spot at all. This isn't where you want. And then she asks: What is this place, is this place a swimming pool?

This is the Gosforth Pool and Fitness Centre, he says.

Where is it you're looking for, love?

Where is it you're looking for, love?

Love, what is it you're looking for?

It's the library I need, I'm looking for the library, I need to get there pretty quick. The red hand jerks on the clock behind him. Well, okay, and he looks at the others, okay, we understand now, so you're not so very far off, if it's Gosforth Library you want, it's Gosforth Library, is it, love? He gets a notepad, spiral, and he draws on it, a tree or a drainpipe, with a rollerball, and the ink dries, goes from shiny to flat. The paper's as white as Jimmy's skin, black writing of the tattoo.

Look, maybe, do you want me to phone somebody? Phone somebody? Like who? I don't know, he says. I don't need you to phone anybody, I just need to get to the library, so thank you very much indeed but no need to be phoning anyone, absolutely not necessary for any phone calls. Love, are you really alright? really alright? Not sure that we shouldn't be phoning somebody, you know. At least phone you a taxi. But you said I'm not far off, not far off the library, do I need a taxi? Taxi would only be ten minutes, take a seat, over there, we'll get you a taxi. No, I can't wait around, I'm already late, but thank you very much indeed, much appreciated, much appreciated.

The page he gave her, she turns it different ways under the streetlamp that sounds louder now. It makes sense, that way, or maybe it doesn't… the rectangle must be the swimming pool but the arrow points towards it. A cluster of cars at the far end of that bare road, so Paula tightens her belt and heads in their direction.

*

A couple of bluebottles have got trapped in the lighting box behind the big neon menu that runs above the counter. All night they'll be buzzing, batting against the plastic, decreasingly frantic. But it'll take them until tomorrow to die. Karim Assif looks at the clock. Outside it's raining again. Quiet now, but it'll be busy before too long. He doesn't like it here, he should never have come, Karim Assif. They had talked it up better than it is. White sky never gives you a break. He thinks instead of the sign, Welcome to Fabulous Las Vegas, Nevada, and he thinks of 24-hour everything: strip clubs, shows, showgirls, the tables, the machines, sunshine non-stop. But he's here. Why are they not back from the cash and carry yet? There was a woman in earlier, big silver alien face, didn't know where she was. Fallen over, cut her leg, crying. Didn't know where she was. He'd pointed in the direction of the station. When he came out from the back she'd gone. Fountains at the Bellagio look cool. The actual fucking volcano at the Mirage. Flies keep on buzzing.

# Lady and Dog

Olga McClure feeds the pencil into the sharpener, turns the handle. There's the wood's slight resistance until it yields to the blade and then the movement runs smooth. She repeats it with another pencil, and then another. It'll need to be done thirty-two times. Olga knows who hovers at the door but she won't look over. A pencil emerges with the lead broken. So do it again.

The bright voice: Olga! Olga, you haven't forgotten our meeting?

I haven't forgotten, she says, not lifting her head.

Well then, Olga, ready when you are. Just in the next ten minutes.


Ms Druggan sits not at her desk but on the comfortable orange seat in the corner. She wears running gear.

Take a seat, Olga, Ms Druggan says, indicating the comfortable green seat. Now, would you like a cup of tea?

No thank you.

Excuse my outfit, she says. I'm in training for a 10K race.

It's for charity, says Ms Druggan.

For charity, says Olga. Very good.

So, Ms Druggan begins, I thought it was maybe a good time for the two of us to have a bit of a chat. You know? A chat about a few things here and there that need to be sorted out. Just a couple of things.

Right.

Yes, says Ms Druggan.

I see.

Ms Druggan sits up straighter. Uh huh, she says.

Tell me this, Olga, she says, when, and I want you to be completely honest, when did you last switch on your computer?

My computer?

Yeah.

Well, Olga says, let me see now. Hard to give a definitive answer. Maybe two weeks ago, possibly a little longer. I'm not sure.

Ms Druggan nods her head. More or less what I thought, she says. Do you feel, Olga, do you feel that you've been given adequate ICT training? Because obviously a computer that hasn't been switched on in two weeks is really not ideal. You know what I mean? Now I absolutely realise that there's a range of staff competence, particularly when it comes to some of the more senior members of staff. Well, senior members of staff in terms of age. I don't underestimate how difficult it can be for some people to embrace new technology. So, maybe you feel you need further support in order to integrate ICT meaningfully.

No. I wouldn't say I require further support.

Well that's good, says Ms Druggan. I'm very glad to hear that. So, to recap, what we're both in agreement on is that it is really really important that you start integrating ICT meaningfully into your teaching. For equality of experience.

Olga sighs. Equality of experience. What a ridiculous idea.

The children in your class, Ms Druggan continues, have not completed the LIN test, which should have been done at the beginning of last week. That's when the children in the other classes completed the LIN test.

Oh. Well.

Yes, says Ms Druggan.

The LIN test is where the pupils have to give the monsters the different types of ice cream. I do know it.

It's a computer-based, standardised cognitive ability assessment.

Well, I'll perhaps pencil it in for next week.

It should have been done at the beginning of last week, if not earlier, says Ms Druggan.

Well, as I said, I will try to see if I can get it done next week.

Another thing, if you haven't switched on your computer in two weeks, do you not feel you've missed a lot of communication?

Olga thinks. Not really, she says.

What do you mean not really?

This is a primary school with eight people working in eight rooms. It's hardly a conglomerate. If anyone needs to speak to me, they know where to find me. And if I need to speak to someone the reverse holds true.

Olga picks up the handbag that has been resting at her feet.

Is that it? she says.

When Olga gets home, the dog is pleased to see her. It yaps as she puts out its food. The small brown thing is always busy, tussling with a rope or chasing a ball. Olga hadn't cared what sort of dog she got. She'd just wanted a dog to take for walks because no one is loitering with a dog. Olga and the dog complete a familiar circuit most evenings so she knows well its favoured lamp posts and the clumps of weeds where it sniffs for whatever's dank and compelling. On Tuesday and Thursday nights their walk extends further to the park, with its wrought iron gates and bandstand, miniature lake and shady paths. She lets the dog off the lead and it heads down the winding ways, always coming back when she calls Dog! She hasn't given it a name. The park route takes Olga and the dog past the playground and the miniature lake but they keep going until they come to the pitches.

The others call Ms Druggan Angie. Angie displays her qualifications and certificates on the wall beside a montage of photos of her and her fiancé on various holidays. She's keen that the staff go out for meals. At Christmas Olga made the concession to go to the dinner which was in an Indian restaurant. She ordered from the European section of the menu, the only one to do so. Old fashioned the others might consider her but there is order in her classroom. Over forty years teaching with well over a thousand children passing through her door. It's the same pole that has been there for all that time, the one to open the high windows, the same cupboard, bleached by the sun, and filled with yellowing, spotted books. Children in the seventies and children in the eighties gazed out those windows longing for the deep blue air, only to be jolted to the here and now by Olga's curt shout of their name. Her desk used to be wooden but the desks were all replaced a few years ago so now it's a toughened laminate. More than a thousand children and she has secretly hated each one at least a bit. There was once a boy she could hardly stand to look at because his eyes were the same, the shape of them. He could have been Eddie's son. The boy's work was always marked too severely and she watched him, puzzled, when he opened the jotter. One day she needed a letter posting and she sent him out down the road in the heavy rain. But I've no jacket, Miss McClure, he said. I've got no jacket with me.

Did you hear what I said? Did you? Go right this minute and no more about it.

He came back shivering with his hair dripping. She could have wrapped her own coat around him. But she said, You're not a sugar lump. You'll live.

Ms Druggan has brought in initiatives which Olga has not embraced: children assessing their own work, children celebrating Chinese New Year, graduation ceremonies for pupils moving on to new key stages, Gaelic football training. Olga has never concealed her disapproval of these projects. She nibbled only the edge of a spring roll at Chinese New Year. When it came to Gaelic football she asked Ms Druggan if the parents had been informed about it because there would be plenty who would take a dim view. Ms Druggan said that yes, of course they'd been informed and not one had raised an objection. But that was probably because the letters from the school had turned to pulp at the bottom of the children's bags, soggy with leaked juice and squashed fruit. Olga had taken it upon herself to bring the Gaelic issue to the attention of George Shields, a mass of muscle and tattoo taught by her when he was nine and skinny. A fortuitous meeting outside the chemist's one day allowed her to ask if Mason, his son, was looking forward to the Gaelic football. George was pretty sanguine.

Where was it happening? Only the school assembly hall? They weren't going to be playing matches anywhere? He shrugged. Well whatever, he had said. At the Frampton-Martinez fight he had had his photo taken with Carl's wife. She was lovely. And she was from the west of the city. It was only the school assembly hall, a bit of exercise. People needed to chill for Christ's sake. It was 2018.

Olga's evenings are usually segmented neatly into half hours: a half hour to read the paper, half hour to work on the pupils' books, to walk the dog, half hour to clean the windows perhaps, half hour to watch a television programme. She sits on her usual seat to eat a slice of potato bread and butter, sprinkled with white sugar. That hand's sweep is quick and smooth: not long until it's half past six and time to go out. She forgot about the bin this morning. The length of her street still had plenty of empty blue bins sitting out when she returned home from school. Bright blue bins in the last dregs of pale light. But she'd forgotten and she knew that she'd forgotten because she'd been thinking about this evening, the park walk. She woke up looking forward to it. She could leave the bin out next week. What did it really matter? It was only ever a quarter full anyway.

It's developed into a reasonable evening. On a night like this plenty of girls will be out on the road, those same girls who five, six years ago sat at a desk in her room, calculating angles and who now are leaning against the windows of the takeaway or the off-licence. Mostly they don't acknowledge her. She's well used to the imperious blanking, finding it almost amusing in its own way. The strained denim of their hot pants, worn even at this time of the year. The legs burnished with fake tan. They look down at their breasts as if to check that they're still there. And then the love bites, those badges proclaiming carnal success, she sees them, those badges worn with pride. Don't they just consider themselves the first to discover it all? The pioneers. You think I don't know, Olga wants to say. You think I don't know about love bites and not on my neck. And the purple and green thumb prints on that fine skin on my hips. A strong, sunburnt, sapling body poured into a tight dress. Well strong becomes stocky as time goes by and a tight dress is passed over in favour of a comfort cut. How could they think she ever knew?

The books are marked already, each with a three line comment in an elegant hand. She did it after school in her room, before sharpening the pencils. Olga wonders about her forgotten password for the computer. She must have written it down somewhere. Olga had thought the dog would shed hairs everywhere but it doesn't. The neighbours she thought might complain about the barking but they don't.

The first time that the Gaelic fellow, Cormac, appeared, Olga deliberately overran her lesson. It was only when Ms Druggan appeared that they had to terminate what they were doing. Cormac the Gaelic fellow had shaken her hand hard when Ms Druggan introduced them. His arms were covered in freckles. He said, I was wondering where yous lads were, if yous were ever going to turn up.

Well, they're here now, Ms Druggan said.

Hey why you not got your trainers on, you not giving it a go yourself?

The question was directed at Olga.

I don't think so, she said without smiling.

Well you better have them next week, he said. Try and find your old school PE kit as well, see if you still fit into it. Probably still knocking about the house somewhere.

Olga had considered going to see Ms Druggan because that was absolute insolence and she did not appreciate it: only in the place five minutes and the Gaelic fellow was already taking liberties. Futile though, Ms Druggan would say it was nothing more than a joke. Olga noted how the pupils enjoyed their session with him, and did what he said without complaint. Balls went bouncing down the hall. Balls went bouncing up the hall. The estate crowd who she'd thought—hoped—might be trouble listened to every word he said. What very little allegiance they had to her was reassigned to the Gaelic fellow within five minutes of flying footballs and beanbags.

She didn't even have a pair of training shoes, never mind a kit. When the children did PE she stood at the side of the assembly hall in her neat, low-heel courts, calling out what they should do. A PE kit from school, the very daftness of it. There was little in the house from her younger days, apart from a few pieces of crockery that had belonged to her mother. On the mantelpiece she used to have that photo of where she grew up but not anymore. The newspaper clipping she had carried in her handbag, had been folded and unfolded so many times that it finally disintegrated into pieces. Snipped out forty-five years ago with the only scissors that were about at the time, the pinking shears with the zig-zag edges. She put the paper in the bin so no one would notice the hole, and query what she was doing. It wasn't much of a photo, the way he stared out serious and startled, although the quality of the likeness was not the major concern at the time.

The day it happened was dull and hot. Olga wore the blue dress, the one he'd said he liked, although it was the kind of day, everything sticking to you, when you'd happily have taken off all your clothes. The hair at her nape was damp and dark. He had said where he was going to be, working in an outhouse, on the way towards the top brae. Going across the river would be easier and not that long way round, the whole distance up to the bridge. The racket of the crickets and all that spit on the long grass: her dress would be soaking with the stuff after going across the fields. Nobody would think anything of seeing her walking along the road, Olga thought, but Eddie had said to be careful even when you don't think you need to be. That's when you most need to be careful.

She had seen him just the once in the town with his wife when they were going into the shoe shop on the corner. The shoe shop. Olga would never have imagined him buying shoes. She couldn't visualise him trying one on, then the other, walking up and down, saying they're a bit tight, have you got a bigger size? But he hadn't seen her in the town and she didn't mention that she had seen him. She didn't say that she waited behind a wall so she could see him and his wife come out of the shop again, with him carrying the bag. He was still wearing the same old boots the next time she saw him. His wife had hair folded up in into a pleat.

She had said to him one time when she was sitting on his lap, Why is it you like me?

Because you're seventeen, he said.

No but why is it really?

Because you're good looking and you're seventeen. He stroked her head.

She punched his arm. Like you're the old man. You're not any more than about five years older. I can even remember when you were at the school.

The school, he groaned. I didn't like the school and the school didn't like me.

What is your new uniform going to look like? she asked. You'll have seen the fellas wearing it.

Yeah, but what do you look like in it? What's the hat like? Why even join? It's not as if you don't already have a job.

Money.

Do you not have enough money?

It wouldn't seem so, he said.

Olga leaves her terraced street with its tidy gardens to head down the curving road, past the old mill converted into apartments. The dog trots along, pulling pleasantly on the lead. I know, Olga says, I know. We'll be there soon. At the entrance to the park a group of kids sit on top of one of the picnic tables, pushing and shoving each other, sharing a bottle of something. Their shrieks and laughs echo in the silence of the evening. The tarmac of the path seems to gleam, the sky is pearly. Funny how she lived near the park for all these years without ever venturing into it. It was just something beyond the railings. She has a memory of someone, a politician, having an assignation in some shady corner there with another man. It was in the papers, she is sure. On some of the park benches people sit on their own.

The next time that Cormac the Gaelic fellow came, Olga ensured that she was there promptly in the assembly hall with the children.

Alright chief, he had said to her. You gonna be giving it

a go today? We gonna see a bit of involvement from you today?

Olga said there were things that she needed to do back in the room. No point in getting too involved in case she had to leave.

He just nodded. Sure, he said. No probs. Next time though!

From the window she watched him leave after the session. He wore a top with the name of something on it. Those curving, tubby letters, that way of writing, she had never really liked it. Somebody had bought her a mug once that had 'coffee' written on it like that and she had put it in the back of the cupboard. Celtic Collection: that was the shop in the town with its sign written like that. She really wouldn't wear anything green. Her least favourite sweet out of the pastilles was the green. Just the way it was. Ms Druggan had seen her in the corridor that afternoon and had asked if everything was going well with Cormac. Olga said that well, there hadn't been any complaints, there hadn't been any complaints so far. Just the way it was. That way of writing though, she's become accustomed to it. That mug it might still be there, right at the back.

There wasn't a person she could tell when it happened. Her mother might well have suspected something or other, Olga had sometimes wondered if she did, but nothing was ever mentioned. If only one soul could just have said well there now, there, or put a quiet hand on her arm. A look from someone, a look even without a smile, a look even half in judgment, it would have been something. She saw his wife again in the town and she despised her and the way she was allowed to have her hair all hanging lank as she went around with the sad old face. The wife didn't know who she was, even though what they felt must have been the equal. The whitewashed wall of the old toilet down in the scullery, it always felt damp to the touch even in the summer; she used to run her finger along it looking for even just a tiny fleck of blood suspended in the wet that would make her breathe the sigh of relief that everything was fine that month. But then, once he wasn't there any more, she was desperate to see it clear, that the finger run on the wall ran clear, so that he would still be with her in a different way. But there it was, rust against the whitewash.

She had thrown herself into her studies and moved to Belfast where the training college was nearly all girls. Most were religious and some had fiancés that they wouldn't let touch them until they were married. Olga cut her hair short. Three brisk strokes of the brush and that was it done. Olga, the vestal virgin who they thought was saving herself for the right man although, they joked, he might be hard to find with hair like that.

Olga wonders, as she passes some majestic chrysanthemums, where exactly the politician met the man and if had they known each other before their meeting. He would have been well advised to choose somewhere down by the old entrance where the trees are thicker, where at some points it edges into total darkness. The park closes at nine o'clock but Olga has seen people climbing over the pronged railings, with shouts and laughter.

Cormac always has some joke or other. Well boss, he said to Olga, what club are you going to be hitting Saturday night? The pupils loved it. Miss McClure like. Going to a club. Don't be so daft, Cormac, honestly, she said. But one week when Olga was in the city centre she looked at what was fly-posted on walls. There was someone or other called Jackmaster plus Jasper James @Sixty6 at the weekend. So when Cormac asked her again the next week, well boss what club are you going to be hitting Saturday night? Olga said, Sixty6. I'm going to listen to Jackmaster and Jasper James.

What? he said.

Jackmaster at the club Sixty6.

Right, he said. Okay. I'm not too sure I know where that is now.

It was only a joke, Olga said. I was just joking.

That's funny, Cormac said. Good joke.

She had helped him put the footballs into the net bags when the bell rang for break.

There was a morning earlier in the year when one of the girls had said, You know who I seen the other night, Miss? I seen you coming into the shop and you bought a paper and a packet of biscuits.

A paper and a packet of biscuits? Olga said. Well now, that could indeed have been me.

One of the boys said, Know what, I saw Cormac the other night and he was doing the stuff that he does with us only there was a man telling him to do the stuff he does with us.

And where might that have been? Olga asked.

That park up near Ravenhill. That place away up there.

That evening, when she had everything done, Olga went to the park. She had to consult the graffitied map covered in burnt plastic to work out a route. It took several circuits past the bandstand before she realised that there were playing fields right at the top. Once there Olga took only swift and surreptitious glances in the direction of the people who were running about. She feigned an interest in the rose bushes near the car park.

A man said to her, Is it the Intermediates you're after?

She hadn't known what to say.

Sorry, he said, I thought you were somebody else. I thought you were somebody's ma.

It took several visits before Olga had the idea about the dog. There was an ad in the local shop for one that needed a home and Olga, as soon as she went into the woman's house and saw it, said, That'll do. That'll do fine. The woman had wanted to give her a cup of tea and tell the whole life story of this dog that used to belong to one of her neighbours. Olga politely said she couldn't stay.

There are only a few teams training this evening. It's getting chillier and the people watching hop from foot to foot to keep warm. There's a van selling burgers and chips, the smell of fried onions in the air, but nobody is buying any. The man in the van is playing country music and it's a song Olga's heard many times over the years without knowing its name or who sings it, a plaintive tale of bad luck and regret. The man in the van looks maudlin as he looks at the burger baps, piled on a tray.

So many sounds, Olga thinks. She can tell within a second if a pupil's cry is genuine or attention-seeking. Anyone can tell it's country from the van within a couple of seconds without being able to say what country really is. No need to be a musical expert. Glass smashes and you know if it's a bottle or a window. You don't need to see. That day she was crossing the big field when she heard the noise, a sound assertive and dull at the same time. Had someone dropped pallets from a height? Little red weals were coming up on her legs from things that had bitten her, and she knew those freckles on her face would be out. Rub them with lemon juice all you want like it says in the magazines, but it wouldn't make them fade. She fixed her dress around the neck so it sat nice, then smoothed down her hair, pressed her lips together. They wrote the songs about this feeling.

She couldn't see him at first. She called his name but sure hadn't he done this before: she'd go around searching for him, and then he'd creep up and catch her hard around the waist. Got you! She nearly wet herself that one time.

Olga shouted but there was no answer.

This was the place and this was the time, where he said and when he said. She wouldn't have made a mistake.

Eddie! she shouted. Eddie! And then another time, even though she felt foolish.

Although he had never been late before, there was always a first time. Couldn't he get held up somewhere, or find it difficult to get away? Stuck in the town, buying another pair of shoes. The shop assistant chatting away as she puts them in the bag and hands him his change.

But over there, by a heap of breeze blocks she saw his legs.

What in the name of goodness are you doing? Olga said. Get up, Eddie! What are you doing?

And then she saw it, the obscenity of an exploded head. A mass of red matter.

Olga began to run, she hardly knew in what direction, and although there was no one to hear she was saying over and over, oh my God oh my God oh my dear God please help me. The quickest way to get back was across the river and not that long way right around. She just jumped in, didn't even feel the water cold. Just ten, twelve strokes across but the water was heavy, muscled, pulling at her legs even though she was kicking hard. She, frantic, and the current pushing her downstream slowly, casually, with no great fuss of noise or foam.

Cormac's a giant in the assembly hall but here at the pitches he always seems slight. Even Olga can see that most of the others are more proficient at handling that ball. A couple of children standing beside her stop to pet the dog. It likes the attention and tangles the lead with twirling. What sort of wee dog is she? the girl asks. I really don't know, Olga says.

These people around her are respectable people, solicitors and doctors most likely. She could go into the club house there, the St Columba's clubhouse and she would probably get a nice cup of tea. The cars in the carpark aren't old jalopies either. She had tried to imagine the man who killed Eddie, man or men. They never got anybody for it. Three weeks later in a town five miles away a boy who worked in the shirt factory was shot dead in retaliation and it was viewed with a sense of inevitability in Olga's house. All sympathy was with the part-time RUC Reservist's wife. Olga's mother sent a stew up to her and a couple of boxes of shortbread, the sombre biscuit. He'd been found by two men who'd been working down the road. It was the day when Olga had taken the head-staggers and fallen into the river, a girl of her age falling into the river, would you believe it? She had turned up dripping at the Alexanders' place, jabbering like a loon about a shooting. Somebody she met on the way must have told her. The Alexanders heard the shot too. Everyone heard the shot.

She's glad she switched on the heat before she left. The coal fire's gone, replaced with the feature heater and its facsimile of glowing embers. The dog sits at her feet. You don't realise how cold it is outside until you come in. Olga wonders where Cormac goes after training. Does he just go home? One of the boys in the class said once, hey Cormac do you have a girlfriend? Olga said, That's none of your business, Jonathan, none of your business whatsoever. But Cormac said, No I don't, Jonathan, but I'm on the lookout. You know anybody decent? When they'd got back to the classroom she'd said to the boy, Don't be asking anything like that again because I'm sure Cormac does not appreciate it.

But he didn't have a girlfriend.

Everyone looks forward to Friday. The bell sounds melodic on a Friday. Olga comes in early in the morning to cut with the guillotine the thirty-two small squares of paper in three different colours that are needed for a maths exercise. She writes a paragraph on the whiteboard, ready for the children to correct its punctuation. They will look at leaves today, horse chestnut, oak and cypress. Some of the children wear trainers on a Friday and they leave their ties at home.

Please don't run, Olga says, when she lets them out to the assembly hall for the session with Cormac. She follows behind them, never appearing eager. He'll be with the class for a whole forty minutes, and then there will be the further five when she helps him tidy up at the start of lunch. She sees the blue and green tracksuit which says St Columba's on the back and the children have gathered around, waiting for orders about what to do next. But then—

Sorry, what's going on? Olga asks.

The young man shakes her hand. Tommy, he says.

But I was expecting Cormac! The children were expecting Cormac.

Well you won't be seeing him for a while.

What do you mean?

That's him away off now, Tommy says.

Where's he away off to? What do you mean?

Now I'm not the best person to be asking, says Tommy. Cos I never pay attention to all the details. He did tell me now. Is it Germany? Or maybe it's Holland. Got one of them engineering jobs.

Are you sure?

Pretty sure it's Germany. If not it's definitely Holland.

Two of the boys are starting to climb up the ropes that hang from the wooden apparatus.

But he was there last night, says Olga. At the training last night.

Yeah we all went out after, says Tommy. Hey, are you a St Columba's woman yourself?

I need to speak to someone about this, says Olga. I actually think this is… this is outrageous.

She walks down the corridor to Ms Druggan's office. There is a Meeting in Progress, Do Not Disturb sign on the door but she knocks anyway. And then knocks again.

What is it, Olga? says Ms Druggan when she opens the door. She steps into the corridor to whisper, Can't you see? I've got people from the board here!

Cormac, you know, the Gaelic fellow, he's been coming for a long time and now, suddenly, completely out of the blue he's gone and there's some other person down in the hall. It's completely unacceptable. Absolutely and totally.

Ms Druggan stares at her.

It's outrageous. The children have got used to him and

then that's it, without any notice, he's not there. Did you know he was leaving?

Look, says Ms Druggan, Olga, the young people who come in, they're just volunteers. They're not being paid and isn't it good they're prepared to come at all, for whatever length of time? I have to go, she says, pointing at the sign on her door.

It's atrocious.

That project's coming to an end anyway. Three more weeks and then it's street dance. The people from the board, Ms Druggan says. They're waiting for me in there. I really do need to get back to the people from the board.

The children have fallen into the same groups they formed when they were with Cormac and they don't notice her coming in. When the session ends, Tommy says that he'll see everyone next week. As the children file out, he phones somebody. Over in the corner Olga watches him. She hears him speaking to somebody, yeah, yeah, no way, ha, yeah, no probs. The children are happy because Friday is chips.

In the afternoon the rain pelts against the classroom window. The children are squirming in the seats, bored by the slow crawl of another Friday afternoon. The room is too hot and the condensation steams up the windows. One of the children has drawn a face in it. A girl asks, Can we watch a DVD this afternoon because the other people get to watch DVDs, but Olga says no, of course not. No DVDs. She can feel the veins throbbing under the thin skin of her temples. The girl says no more, resigning herself to the photocopied arithmetic problems, numbered 1 to 24. With only three quarters of an hour to go, Olga takes the class to the computer room to do the test Ms Druggan had talked of. She doesn't even need to know a password because the pupils can access the application without her input. The children silently feed the monsters different flavours of ice cream in various combinations and occasionally there is a peal of bleeps when someone unlocks a new level. In the computer room the blinds are always drawn. Then they go back to the classroom for their coats and bags and to wait for the bell. Put up your chairs, Olga shouts. Put up your chairs before you go. Although weary, she sharpens the pencils again, sorts the jotters alphabetically so that when she marks them later they'll be in order. She wipes off the window the face drawn by the child.

When Olga puts her key in the door, she hears the dog, its excited, impatient barks. Her jacket is wet so she hangs it over the radiator. She'll need to bring out the winter coat soon. Olga takes off her shoes, rubs her feet. You don't realise they're even sore until the shoes are off. In her bedroom she puts her blouse and skirt on the hanger, closes the wardrobe. Her dressing gown hangs on the hook on the back of the bedroom door.

The dog is hungry so she pours out the dry feed and sits at the table with a cup of tea, watching it finish its bowl, tail wagging. Street dance anyway, in another few weeks' time. She could go upstairs and run a bath, both taps on full, the water stilling and thickening as it edges higher. She imagines the dog, its panic, its frantic heart as it fights against the water, and the impotent movement of its paws.

# 77 Pop Facts You Didn't Know About Gil Courtney

1. Gillespie Stanley John Courtney was born in Belfast on July 26th 1950. Also born on July 26th were Aldous Huxley, Jason Robards and Kevin Spacey.

2. Gil Courtney's mother, Elsie, registered him with her maiden name—Gillespie—as his Christian name. She initially said that this was done in error but in later years admitted that it was intentional.

3. Gil Courtney grew up at 166 Tildarg Street, Cregagh, Belfast. Some of the lyrics to the song 'Partial Aperture' on the first The Palomar album, *Golden Dusk*, are often said to have been inspired by the view from the back bedroom of this house. Visible beyond the rooftops are the Castlereagh Hills.

4. Palomar were known as The Palomar until 1975. Thereafter, they were known as Palomar.

5. The phrase 'taking drugs to make music to take drugs to', later used as the title of a Spacemen 3 album, was reputedly first coined by Gil Courtney during the recording of *Golden Dusk*.

6. The front room of the house at 166 Tildarg Street had a silver disc above the mantelpiece. (Although *Golden Dusk* only reached 21 in the UK charts, European sales ensured its silver status.) Gil recalled on a trip home one time taking it off the wall and playing it. 'And what do you think it was,' he said when interviewed in 1972, 'but an Alma Cogan record dipped in silver paint. The paint just flaked off on my hands.'

7. It is likely that Gil Courtney's father was not Alec Courtney, husband of Elsie, and clerk at James Mackie and Sons, Belfast. Elsie was five months pregnant when they married. She was of the opinion that the father was most probably a merchant seaman, possibly Spanish, whom she met in Dubarry's Bar (now McHughs).

8. 166 Tildarg Street was on the market in 2012. The estate agent's description pointed out that it was in need of some modernisation. Photos showed empty rooms, bare walls and floorboards. Elsie Courtney's furniture and carpets had been removed to a skip some weeks earlier.

9. Gil Courtney's first instrument was the xylophone. At primary school a new teacher who introduced a musical half-hour on a Friday afternoon was surprised to see one of her pupils playing two xylophones at once. The young Gil Courtney said he was able to remember the tune of something he'd heard on the radio.

10. Miss Kathleen Hughes, a P7 teacher and church organist, gave Gil Courtney piano lessons in the school assembly hall. She later said that she had never encountered a child with such exceptional ability and whose sight-reading was so extraordinary. When Kathleen Hughes was unable to attend a funeral service owing to illness the eleven-year-old Gil took her place at the organ.

11. Gil Courtney's girlfriend, Simone Lindstrom, went on to have brief relationships with Neil Young and Terry Melcher, son of Doris Day. Dicky Griffin of Palomar described Simone as a 'high-maintenance kind of chick', while Elsie Courtney said she was 'Simone with the little turnip tits in the polo necks you could spit through.'

12. When Gil Courtney was fifteen he began playing with many of the showbands popular in Northern Ireland at the time. He played in groups including The Buccaneers, The Dakotas, The College Boys and The Emperors. Two or three gigs a week would have been common. Ronnie O'Hanlon, drummer in The Dakotas, recalled how they would travel across the province in the back of a van with the equipment: 'A lot of the roads were bad and you were thrown all over the place. A lot of these places were in the middle of nowhere. The driver'd be thinking where in the name of God are we going down this dirt track and then all of a sudden, out of the dark there would be a dancehall, all lit up.'

13. Gil Courtney's music lessons with Miss Hughes always began with the removal of the boxes of sports equipment stacked on top of the piano.

14. The fourth song from Gil Courtney's solo album, *Volonte Blue*, was played by Stuart Maconie on his programme *The Freak Zone* on 6 Music on Sunday 16th October 2011.

15. In the Oh Yeah Music Centre in Belfast there is a small exhibition of Northern Irish pop memorabilia. There is a photograph of Gil Courtney and other members of The Palomar taken outside Gideon Hall's flat in London. They are dressed in the fashions of the time. To the left there is a photo of David McWilliams and to the right a snap of 60s Belfast psychedelic-blues group Eire Apparent.

16. Gil Courtney was educated at Harding Memorial Primary School and Park Parade Secondary School.

17. Gil Courtney used the Hohner Cembalet, the Hammond organ and the Wurlitzer electric piano.

18. Before its eventual closure in 1969, Gil Courtney and other members of both The Dakotas and The Emperors played Hamburg's Star Club. They were part of a group of musicians who briefly went to Germany to 'try their luck'; it was the first time that most of them had been outside Northern Ireland. Gil sent numerous postcards home and Elsie Courtney said that from the spelling and the grammar it was

obvious this was a young man who had not spent long enough in school.

19. In *Uncut* magazine's April 2016 feature, 'The Quest for Rock's Great Lost Albums on Vinyl', Gil Courtney's album *Volonte Blue* was listed at number 13. At number 12 was Linda Perhacs' *Parallelograms.*

20. Alec Courtney, Elsie's husband, always used the name Stanley when referring to Gil.

21. In 1968 Gil Courtney moved to London to work as a session musician, supplementing his wages by joining the house bands at the Dorchester and Park Lane Hotels. 'I never regretted any of my time spent playing in the *palais* bands,' Gil was quoted as having said. 'Many of those guys could really play and I learnt a lot.' During the time that Gil played at the Dorchester, Elsie Courtney and her sister Nan came to London. They stayed in a Dorchester suite, which Gil's connection in reception had managed to secure them *gratis*. 'It was all fine,' Elsie remembered, 'just as long as we always went in the back entrance and up the service stairs and didn't come down for the breakfast.' The sisters danced in the grand ballroom when Gil was playing. 'It was lovely,' Elsie said. 'All the crystal lights. There was a conductor. You should've seen the way the women were dressed. They were beautiful.'

22. The first twenty seconds of the song 'Under the Mountain' from *Golden Dusk* was used as the title

music for an Argentinian football programme for five years in the 1980s. Gil Courtney had a co-writing credit on this and therefore received royalties, along with those for his contribution to several other songs on the record.

23. For a period of time 166 Tildarg Street was a popular destination for those bands who were playing Belfast and did not want to stay in a hotel. Elsie Courtney had fond memories of some of the people who stayed with her. Her favourite was Steve who could still sing the songs from *Oliver!*, the West End show in which he performed as a child. She said that he gave a rendition of 'Consider Yourself' in the kitchen, singing the final chorus up on the table.

24. Steve Marriott's band, The Small Faces, borrowed Gil Courtney's electric piano when they played the Floral Hall in Belfast. Ian McLagan's piano was not playing properly. The Floral Hall, an art deco ballroom overlooking Belfast, is now in disrepair and is used to store animal feed for the nearby zoo.

25. Gil Courtney was 6 feet 1 inch tall. His shoe size was 10.

26. Gideon Hall from Palomar published his autobiography in 2005. It was translated into nine languages.

27. Gil Courtney's work as a session musician brought him into contact with a drummer Kevin Heyward

who had recently joined a band with two guitarists he had met through a mutual friend. Kevin Heyward invited Gil Courtney along to rehearse. This was the birth of The Palomar.

28. Gil Courtney rarely wore any colour other than black.

29. Alec Courtney did not approve of rock and roll, Gil's career or the guests who sometimes arrived at Tildarg Street. Elsie remembered him as an 'old stick in the mud who was happier down at the bible study.'

30. Gideon Hall was rather scathing about Elsie Courtney whom Gil would occasionally bring over for shows in London and Glasgow. 'God spare us all from the living embodiment of the oral tradition,' he was quoted as saying. 'What are the words guaranteed to strike most dread in me? *The motherfucking mother's here.*'

31. During breaks in session work, Gil Courtney would read paperbacks, usually either Agatha Christie or American sci-fi stories. 'Simone tried to get me into poetry, Ginsberg and so on, but I never really dug it.'

32. In his autobiography, Gideon Hall said of Courtney, 'I daresay it sounds harsh, perhaps it is, but really, was he anything more than a footnote? If even that? The myth of the beautiful loser. It's tired. It's tiresome.'

33. Gil Courtney went on a trip to Marrakech with a group of friends including Brian Jones of The Rolling

Stones, shortly before the latter's death. Popular amongst the crowd was the local *kif*. Elsie couldn't remember whether Brian Jones had ever come to Tildarg Street. 'All these fellas, the girls might have had them on their walls but if they seen what I seen in the morning, dirty pants and them stinking of sweat and what have you, they might have thought different.'

34. *Golden Dusk* was described optimistically and ultimately accurately by Charles Shaar Murray as a 'prelude to greatness.' It received generally positive reviews in *Melody Maker* and *New Musical Express*, with critics particularly praising the Gideon Hall / Dicky Griffin-penned 'Goldline' and 'Damascus'. The songs on which Gil Courtney had co-writing credits were noted for their 'somewhat baroque excess.'

35. 'Goldline' was released as a single. It got to number 34 in the British charts but fared rather better in France. The band had a promo slot on a French television programme in 1972, the first one minute and twenty-three seconds of which can be viewed on YouTube. Gil Courtney for most of this time is just out of shot.

36. When Gideon Hall's autobiography was published it was selected by Eason's for inclusion on their roster for priority in-store promotion. Elsie Courtney was reprimanded by a member of Eason's staff in Donegall Place for moving some of the Gideon Hall books off the prominent display.

37. In January 1973 there was a drugs bust at Gil Courtney's Pimlico flat where a party was in progress. The raid allegedly discovered grass, cannabis resin and Mandrax tablets. Owing to Gil Courtney's apparent medical problems, a psychiatrist was able to make the case that he should receive a suspended sentence. It meant, however, that Courtney was unable to obtain a visa to tour overseas.

38. In a Q&A in *Pop Starz* magazine in the same year Gil Courtney answered the following: Favourite food? Ice cream and jelly. Favourite drink: tea. Favourite colour: yellow. Favourite way to spend a day: going for a walk in the park with friends. Favourite type of girl: nice.

39. In a 1993 interview, Van Morrison was asked if he could remember Gil Courtney. He said no.

40. Gil Courtney had a phobia of flying which he tried to alleviate through alcohol and drug use. Even a short flight would induce a panic attack. On a flight to France in 1972 he was unconscious when the group landed at Charles de Gaulle airport. He made the return journey by land and sea, arriving in London approximately two weeks later. Elsie Courtney said that she could never understand Gil's fear of airplanes. 'Well I don't know,' she said. 'What in the name of God's the problem? How could you not like it? I love getting on a plane. I love the drinks and the food in the little compartments and I love the air-hostesses and I love the duty-free.'

41. Gil Courtney failed to turn up for two concerts, one at Glasgow Barrowlands and the other at Manchester Free Trade Hall. The Palomar's manager at the time, Lenny Enlander, was dispatched to the Pimlico flat to tell Gil that he no longer had a place in the group. Enlander said later that 'It was hard to tell if Gil was actually there. Some guy I'd never seen before opened the door. It was like a *tabagie*. Smoke-filled. With blackout curtains on every window. I didn't want to tell him with other people there but Gil didn't want to leave and they didn't want to leave. I just said that's it, Gil. You can't go on. He didn't seem all that bothered. But then I didn't know if he entirely understood what I was saying, if you know what I'm saying.' Lenny Enlander did not stay in music management. He ended up running a successful imports-exports business off the Great Eastern Road.

42. The web-based T-shirt business Avalanche Tees printed a limited run of T-shirts bearing the front cover of *Volonte Blue* after the feature in *Uncut*. These were available on Amazon and eBay later, at a reduced price. One of the T-shirts was sent to Texas.

43. Studio musicians who worked on *Volonte Blue* were unanimous in declaring the process tortuous. Courtney expected them to work up to twenty hours a day yet there were also periods when he would disappear for hours at a time and they would be left to their own devices. 'After the, what, fiftieth take, I was finished,' bass player Mac McLean said. 'I have worked with some picky bastards but the man was

just insane. Charming for sure, but insane. "Play this like a peach being placed on a terracotta tile. In Marrakech." You know? Impossible.'

44.   Gil Courtney and Simone Lindstrom were described in one magazine at the time as 'the most photogenic couple in London.' The magazine featured a photo of the pair in a sitting room with an ornately corniced high ceiling; Simone was in a filmy white dress and reclining on a sofa smoking a cigarette while Gil was crouched in front of her in a black suit. The picture could be regarded as a chilly version of Dylan's *Bringing It All Back Home* cover. The accompanying article profiled the couple in some detail and stated that Gil Courtney's imminent solo album was eagerly awaited.

45.   The artwork for *Volonte Blue* features a striking image of an animal (non-specific) lying dead in the middle of a blue desert. Responsible for the cover was Peter Christopherson of the design group Hipgnosis and later of the band Throbbing Gristle.

46.   The song 'Tint', the lead track on Side 2 of *Volonte Blue* was said by Gil to have been inspired by cellophane sweet wrappers.

47.   When Alec Courtney died of a heart attack in 1975, Gil Courtney was unable to return home for the funeral.

48.   The reception *Volonte Blue* received was lukewarm.

Some critics praised the '*naif* charm' of some of its lyrics and others its 'loosening of formal structures' but for many listeners it was characterised by incoherence and indulgence. Gil's health-related issues meant that the tour to promote the album had to be postponed, and then eventually cancelled.

49. The Palomar's second album, *CCS*, regularly makes it on to lists of the top 50 albums ever recorded. Gil Courtney, interviewed in *Melody Maker* in 1975, was asked if he had listened to *CCS*. After a pause he said, 'Yes, I have.' And then he was asked if he thought it was as good as everyone seemed to think it was. Gil took a long drag on his cigarette. And then he slowly exhaled. 'Yes,' he said. 'It's that good. What else can I say?'

50. In 1978 Gil Courtney played two shows with The Only Ones.

51. Gil Courtney returned to Belfast in 1980. It was no longer viable for him to remain in London. He travelled to Stranraer by train and got the ferry to Larne. Elsie Courtney met him at the station at York Road and was alarmed for several reasons. 'Well, first thing,' she said, 'he had no suitcase with him or anything like that, just a plastic bag with a few things in it.' She was also shocked by his skeletal appearance because at that point in his life he was eight and a half stone.

52. A three-second sample from 'Choler', the third song

on Side 1 of *Volonte Blue* was used as a loop by the Dutch DJ Lars van Tellingen in 2001.

53. When Gil was a child, he and Elsie regularly used to visit the waterworks in North Belfast and feed the swans.

54. Gil Courtney had various food obsessions. Elsie Courtney stated that when he returned to Belfast he only wanted to eat food that was white. After a diet for some months of only potatoes, pasta and rice he then decided he only wanted to eat food that wasn't white.

55. In 1989 a student film society at the University of Leeds was making a vox-pop programme to be shown on student network television. The production team stopped random people in the street to ask them what music was important to them and why. The fifth person they filmed on a morning in April was a man, mid-thirties, balding, in a grey jacket. 'The music that means most to me,' he said, 'well, right then, the music that means most to me is without a doubt the music of Gil Courtney who played with The Palomar. His music is for me just, just transporting.' He paused but the camera was still pointed at him so he continued. 'It just, what it does is, it just—penetrates to the heart of what it means to be lonely, or in love or to feel a failure and so, and so, at times I've found great comfort in his music, well, *Volonte Blue* is what I'm talking about really, not so much any of the other stuff he was involved with

at all really, but other times you know I've found it exhilarating and a total affirmation of what it is to be alive. And I am not really overstating that, I do feel that. There's warmth there and there's strangeness there.' He paused again. 'That enough?' The man, embarrassed, laughed, blinked his eyes and put down his head. 'Right then, I think that probably is enough.'

56. For Christmas each year Elsie bought Gil a black merino wool crew-neck sweater.

57. When living again in Tildarg Street, Gil Courtney had a gramophone player and a few records that he played on very low volume. Elsie Courtney said that when you went into the room you wouldn't even have known anything was playing, if you hadn't seen the record rotating.

58. Elsie said that Gil never watched the television. He would only listen to the radio.

59. Gil Courtney used a EMS Putney VCS 3, generally regarded as the first portable analogue synthesiser.

60. A group of teenage girls were interviewed in 1971 for a German magazine's piece on the London music scene. Viv Vallely, 17, said, 'Of all the guys in all the bands the one I like the most is Gil Courtney from The Palomar. He's not like the singer or anything, he just plays the piano thing, but he's so handsome. And I love the way he speaks cos it's Irish and my

granny is Irish. He spoke to me and my friends once when we was waiting outside.'

61. For fifty years the 'house next door', 168 Tildarg Street, was occupied by Arthur McCourt, who was quoted as saying, 'There is something to be said, I really do believe, for being ordinary and having no great talent at anything. I would really wonder if it would have been better for that fella to have gone into a job just like his father, gone to work at Mackie's or wherever, got married, had a couple of kids than go like a firework then nothing. In fact worse than nothing cos I saw the state of him. And for what? What's he got to show, some tunes nobody listens to?'

62. Late one evening in November 1990, as Gil was making his way to the Co-op on the Cregagh Road for cigarettes, he was the victim of robbery and assault. His wallet was stolen and he sustained a broken jaw and a four-inch cut to the side of his head.

63. From 1981 to 1996 Gil Courtney had a repeat prescription for opiate analgesics. Elsie Courtney, who was a patient at another GP practice, supplemented this with a supply of Tramadol, obtained despite her own very good health.

64. Gil Courtney was an aficionado of a magazine entitled *Seven Wonders of the Ancient World* that came out in 1994. Each monthly issue included a scale model of a particular construction. Issues one and

two were The Great Pyramid of Giza and the Temple of Artemis at Ephesus. By issue three, however, few newsagents stocked the title, and Elsie Courtney visited numerous shops around Belfast to find that month's issue. The Lighthouse of Alexandria, issue 4, was found in the newsagent in Queen's Arcade, minus the model component.

65. Old bandmate Gideon Hall appeared on the Sunday Times Rich List in 2010, but did not feature in subsequent years owing to poor property investments.

66. Neighbour Arthur McCourt said that when Gil Courtney died all the life went out of Elsie. 'That was it for her. She'd lived for the fella. There wasn't a lot of point for her after that.'

67. Gil Courtney never learned to drive.

68. The vox-pop filmed by the students from Leeds University, where a passer-by talked about Gil Courtney, did not make it to the final programme because a passing bus rendered the sound too poor in quality.

69. In the later years of his life, Gil Courtney would get up at dawn and walk to the centre of the town. When the buses bringing in students, schoolchildren and workers arrived at City Hall he would walk back home again.

70. The instruments on *Volonte Blue* were the following: harmonica, bass, violin, oboe, guitar, drums, organ, keyboards, synthesiser and mandolin.

71. In Gil Courtney's room he always wanted a bare light bulb. 'I would say to him there's nice lampshades in the town,' Elsie said, 'but he said no, he liked staring up at the filament. He liked the way it glowed.' She added, 'I'd rather have the place half decent but Gil was Gil.'

72. The first record Gil Courtney ever bought was 'Battle of New Orleans' by Lonnie Donegan.

73. When Gil Courtney received his diagnosis he opted not to receive any treatment, since chemotherapy would prolong life by only a few months. In the final days when Elsie could no longer look after him, he was moved to the hospice on the Somerton Road. On his windowsill at the place there was an amaryllis, just coming into bloom, Elsie remembered.

74. A journalist who interviewed The Palomar just after the release of *Golden Dusk* said, 'Tensions were pretty palpable. Gil was funny and intense and very likeable, but he was unpredictable and in some ways utterly clueless. They—Gideon and Dicky—they were very assured, public school background, with all that entails. Kevin was just the drummer. Gil was hardly the boy from the back streets but he was a destabilising element that they wanted to jettison. And Gil made it easy for them with the way

he behaved. Gideon and Dicky, they might have the counter-cultural credentials, but on another day, with another roll of the dice, they could well have ended up in charge of ICI or BP. They were those sorts of people. The juggernaut that Palomar became would tend to bear that out.'

75. Gil Courtney's funeral took place in the Chapel of Rest on the Ravenhill Road. It was attended by only a handful of people, including a former member of The Dakotas and one of The Emperors. Elsie Courtney, in the belief that there would be a record player, had brought a battered and scratched copy of *Volonte Blue* but there was only a CD player available. Ronnie O'Hanlon had a couple of compilation CDs in his car, one of which was *Feelin' Good Vol. 1*, free with the *Daily Mail*. A decision on a track was quickly made. As they filed out of the chapel, 'Everybody's Talkin' by Harry Nilsson was played, the music from *Midnight Cowboy*.

76. Gillespie Stanley John Courtney died in Belfast on February 2nd 2001. Fred Perry, Gene Kelly and Bertrand Russell also died on February 2nd.

77. Gil Courtney's favourite cigarettes were Chesterfields.

# The soul has no skin

Guys who've messed up and gone off track, they'll work in the place for a while, but once the boredom seeps in, they'll get themselves sorted out with something else. Years later a guy like Phil will call in to buy something, a car seat for the baby say, and it'll be, Barry, you still here mate?

Yeah I'm still here.

Said with a smile, a smile and a shrug, because it isn't that bad. It can be a laugh when you do the thing where you pick what you hope to be the most obscure item from the catalogue, and if anyone orders it you have to pay all the others a fiver. Has to be pricey enough because otherwise somebody could get one of their pals to come in and buy the thing so you have to shell out. And it has to be something that could reasonably be ordered and picked up in the shop. Dishwashers or tumble dryers are out. A Scuderia Ferrari Men's XX Yellow Black Chrono Watch maybe. Or a Haven Fresh HF710 Humidifier—Black. A Tefal ActiFry Fryer—Silver. Barry's had a good streak so far with the Flower Flush 8-Light Ceiling Fitting; he picked it over eighteen months ago.

People steal stuff from the shop, as you'd expect. A box

is brought to the collection point for a customer, but then it gets swiped before anyone has a chance to do anything. The security guard in tassels and epaulettes stands at the door. He says the trousers are cut that tight he can hardly move in them. That security guard always seems to be at the other end of the shop when it happens. People settle themselves on the display sofas like it's their own personal living room in the city centre. Bring a packet of biscuits, why don't you. Kick off your shoes and get yourself comfortable. I'm putting the kettle on, anybody want a cup of tea?

Fair amount of hassle some days. The product doesn't work and they want a refund. Some old guy hands you over a toaster that doesn't work, and when you take it, a load of crumbs drop out the bottom. Sir, I am sorry but since you've used this, I can't just give you a refund. You haven't used it? You both stare at the crumbs, saying nothing, before you sweep them off the counter with the back of your hand. Uh huh, uh huh, I do hear what you're saying, but I'm sorry I can't give you a refund. I don't make up these rules. The best I can do, Barry says, is to send it back to the manufacturer for you. No, I don't know how long that would take. Not too sure about that. If I could give you a new toaster, I would, he says, because if he could give them a new toaster he would. The old guy looks murderous.

A bank of ten sleek tellies on the shop floor, the repeated image crisp and saturated. In the staffroom out the back there's a radio, a kettle and a microwave. Barry'd rather mooch around the town for half an hour in the lunch break, smoke a fag in the lane, rather than go to the staff room. Even by two o'clock the town feels tired like it can't be bothered with the afternoon either and longs for the shutters down.

Some of the others, Phil and all that, sometimes say after work to come for a drink, just the one, like. But he'd prefer to get back to the flat. Not much to see at his place. Living room bedroom kitchen bathroom. Bathroom's full of his creams: Vitamin D analogues, corticosteroids. Flakeybake they called him in school, Flakemeister. Slather on the skin stuff morning and night, just one of the things you have to do. Walls here are wafer thin and he hears his neighbours fighting, sometimes: she goes guttural, he goes squeaky. They throw things about before they make up and Barry sees them heading out somewhere, the woman's hand in the back pocket of the fella's jeans. They're alright; they lent him a corkscrew when Annie brought wine one time. And if they find his music annoying, they've never said anything. They're not bad at all.

Annie looked around the place and declared, well, Barry, you haven't exactly embraced the concept of interior decor. *Grand Designs*, this ain't. Alright, the flat's pretty spartan, can't deny it. There's only one thing on the wall, a picture torn out of a magazine of a Gibson Les Paul guitar, bleached pale because it's near the kitchen window and that spot always catches the sun. Barry used to play the guitar, messed around on it anyway, a good few years ago now.

Annie had been one of the bosses for a while, an unusually well-liked one. Everybody knew she drank, but they didn't care because she wasn't operating heavy machinery nor was she personally responsible for any individual's safety. It was never a massive problem that she often had to be busy with administrative tasks out the back until after midday. Only a shop after all, where everyone was an adult. In her younger days she had been into the whole rock scene and she still dressed in that style all the years later: poodle perm, floaty scarves, a biker jacket although now she went with cheap, fake leather. They called her rock hen. Phil started it, then everyone else joined in. Never mind those there rock chicks, here's the rock hen. She'd liked it though, thought it was funny. Annie was married to some Scottish fella who had one of those illnesses where basically everything shuts down slowly over time. Annie said he used to be in the Hell's Angels, except his crowd were called the Blue Angels.

The first time Annie and Barry got together was after a late-night Thursday in the run-up to Christmas. Town was tinselled up with rain and lights and they swigged from a bottle of brandy near the waterfront. Cold enough down there so the brandy was welcome. Back at his place they were leaning on the door as he tried to find the lock and when it opened they tumbled into the dark hall. How long had he lived there and he couldn't find the light switch! In the bedroom he did know where the switch was, but he didn't put it on.

There was another time when they both had a day off and she came around at about half ten in the morning with a bottle of wine.

Is it not meant to be maybe a coffee and a biscuit at this time of the day? Barry said.

According to what? Annie replied. *Barry Young's Guide to Modern Living*?

They borrowed the corkscrew and because he didn't have any wine glasses they drank out of mugs. The rock hen was just a bird with nowhere where you couldn't feel the bones, whereas he seemed to himself a crude and hulking lump. Barry didn't feel guilty. Why should he? It was nothing to do with him, nothing at all, the husband in the wheelchair or whatever it was. He had a fleeting thought of him surrounded by wires and monitors, a skeletal ghoul in motorbike leathers.

Afterwards, when they were lying there, Annie's hand reached out to touch his hip.

Barry, she said. Come on. It's really not that bad. Seriously. It's not.

Yeah, sure, he said. And he reached for his T-shirt and trousers squashed at the bottom of the sofa.

She looked around the room. You know what it's like in here, it's like a monastic cell, she said.

Just the way it is, he said.

Well if it suits you.

It does—you live in a palace yourself? he asked.

You know I don't. You know I don't, Barry.

She half put on her top and then took it off again. She wasn't wearing a bra. Look at me, she said. I want you to look. You see the, well, I hardly need to point any of it out to you, I would rather not give you chapter and verse here, but what you are looking at is not really babe material. What's in front of you isn't exactly a hot piece of ass. Barry. You taken a look? Look.

There's nothing wrong with you, he said.

Course there is, she said. And then she did put on her top, and her jacket. She needed to go. Someone was looking after her husband for a few hours, but she needed to get back so that they could head on. Her time was up.

Barry's morning routine: out of bed, do the creams, get dressed, get a takeaway coffee from the garage, get on the bus. It's the same people, more or less, on the bus each day. Tinny beat of that guy's cheap headphones, the woman always doing her make-up. Some, like him, are tagged with the logos of their work. The uniform's alright. A polo shirt with a sweatshirt for the winter. When he gets off the bus and walks around, he always has at least ten minutes to spare.

Barry has a usual spot for a smoke. He sees his own cigarette butts when he looks down. Looks up and there are empty rails for clothes on the first floor of the building opposite. Beside him the hoardings surrounding a vacant space are covered in weathered, flaking posters. Building on the space was meant to start months ago. They advertise long past club nights, a psychic who visited a hotel on the outskirts of town.

This morning there's been a big delivery so that means lots of stuff for them to unpack. They have to slice through the cardboard and ties with blades. Some of the other guys were there early this morning for the van coming through. You need to go on a day course if you want to be able to unload the lorry, but Barry hasn't attended it, nor does he want to. The new manager won't be around for much longer because he is looking to move to a bigger shop. It's alright unpacking the stuff: you get into a rhythm as you work away. You think about things. Don't think about things. Think about things. Barry goes through the track listing of various albums, tries to remember the back cover of *Second Helping*, Lynyrd Skynyrd, the guitar listing. That new woman on the bus, Polish maybe, the line of her jaw as she wiped a circle in the condensation on the window, but now it's Annie and he feels her leaning against him and laughing as they tumble in his front door. Don't switch on the light.

\*

But didn't everyone say the sun was great for clearing up your skin? The good old sun works wonders. Lying in the park, first summer after he'd started tech, trying to see if everyone was in fact right and that the sun could work some magic. He was down by the old bandstand on one of those early July days of melting tarmac and yellow grass. There were a few fellas from the college going through the park. They came over, sat down for a while, then headed off. They were going off to a party that night.

You wanna come?

No. You're alright.

You sure? What the fuck's the point just hanging around here by yourself?

Hot, hot day. The guys from tech ambled off, but then another bunch came and started throwing a frisbee to each other not far from where he was lying. When the frisbee hit him for the second time, he thought about the cool of the kitchen and going home.

Two playgrounds in the park, one at each entrance. The new one had a zip line and fresh rides, the old a rusty climbing frame and forlorn couple of tyres.

Hey, she shouted when Barry was walking past. Hey there, can you help me?

A girl was dangling there in the old playground, fat legs a few feet off the ground. She was maybe nine or ten. Her hands clung to the rusty bar above her and she couldn't get free because she was hooked to a broken pole by her pants. Face shiny from crying and the sun. Barry reached up and freed her. He held out his hands so that she could take them and jump down.

What happened you? he said. How you get stuck?

203

They'd all been messing around, she said, but then one of her big brothers had gone and done that to her. They'd all cleared off on her after that.

My brothers are always doing stuff like that on me, she said. They have me tortured.

She fixed her skirt, which had got all twisted, pulled up her socks.

Well, Barry said. That's you down now anyway. He felt around in his pocket and found a 50p.

Take it sure, he said. Get yourself something. Away on, off you go and get yourself something. Get an ice cream or some sweeties.

She took the coin and walked off towards the gates, breaking into a skip as she got closer.

Did none of yous think when you were unpacking all this stuff that there seemed to be a bit of an excessive amount for us? James the manager says. None of yous boys think about that?

Some of the stuff they have just unpacked should have gone to the other shops. They are overwhelmed with ironing boards.

Not really, Barry says.

Nah, never thought, Phil says. You told us to unpack the stuff, so that's what we did.

Well I'm gonna have to arrange for them to be taken away again, James says. So don't be doing anything more with those ironing boards.

They stack them in the only empty space in the store and get back to unpacking more stuff, but James comes back through again and tells Phil that he needs him out the front. Annie always said, would you mind, in work.

Would you mind giving me a hand. Would you mind coming out the front. Nobody ever did mind. When Annie didn't appear in work for the best part of a month nobody knew what had happened. Barry tried to phone her but there was never any answer. One night he was going to bed when she appeared at his door. How could you be skinny and bloated at the same time? She said she wouldn't stay long, she'd come in for just a minute or two. He made a couple of cups of tea in the mugs where they'd once had the wine.

When you coming back? Barry asked. Place is going to wrack and ruin without you.

Oh yeah, right enough.

Yeah. We got all these temporary managers, haven't a clue. Everybody misses you big time.

She said that she wouldn't be coming back to work again because it had all got too much.

You know what I'm talking about, she said.

He asked if they were moving her somewhere else.

I don't think so, Barry, she said. There comes a time when I think you just have to call it a day.

Well, said Barry, yeah. Suppose so.

I do though, he said, I do miss you.

Yeah well. Something for you, she said. It was a set of glasses. They were popular those glasses because they only cost £8.99. They were the four pack Belgravia wine glasses 38cl. On the cardboard there was a soft focus shot of a pretty woman holding one of the glasses to her lips. Barry knew he and Annie probably wouldn't see each other again unless by chance.

Thanks, he said. I'll make sure that these are used next time I've got somebody around for a drink.

Well, Barry, Annie said, I would love to hear that you were using those glasses.

Back from the park the house was still and dark as he knew it would be, and the water from the tap tasted so cold. After tea he was lying on his bed listening to something or other with the headphones on when his ma opened his door.

You need to get downstairs, she said. Quick, Barry.

Why?

There's a policeman! she said. She was untying her apron, fixing her hair in the mirror on the landing.

The police?

Yes. You better go down, Barry. What on earth's it about? They want to speak to you. You haven't even got your shoes on, where's your shoes?

Here's Barry now, his dad said when he came to the door. The policeman was young and smiling. He said that all they needed was just a quick chat with him, wouldn't take long at all they hoped.

Me?

The policeman nodded.

You need to speak to me?

Had there been a terrible crime that he'd not noticed himself witnessing? He didn't know anybody that got in trouble with the police. One of the fellas from tech that he saw earlier had been smoking a bit of grass in the park. Had somebody seen that? Was that what it was?

He asked the policeman what happened. Was it something he'd done?

The policeman was pleasant. He smiled. We just would like you to attend the police station for the purposes of assisting us with an investigation, he said.

Excuse me, sir, are you arresting Barry? his dad asked.

Oh no, we're asking him to attend the station voluntarily.

His mum came down the stairs holding his old school shoes. The policeman watched him as he put them on. Old school shoes and jeans. He felt suspicious already.

In the car the bulk in the front seat was another policeman. He said nothing when Barry got in and the three of them drove along in silence. Then the car stopped at a garage. The young one went in to get something so it was just Barry and the other one in the car. He turned around slowly and deliberately to give Barry a long stare. He put down the window and spat onto the garage forecourt before giving a weary sigh. Barry started to rub at one elbow and then the other.

They turned out of the garage and drove back down the way that they had come. They passed the bottom of his road and suddenly it looked beautiful. The sun was hazy in the trees and there was a guy out washing his car, clots of suds gleaming on the road. Barry thought how he never knew before that he loved that road. It was just the road. All those people at the bus stop. You could see the cranes and beyond them the hills. The adverts in the estate agent's window set out in a grid, all those little houses, he loved everything about it, and the people coming out of the Chinese with their takeaway. It was all so fragile, who would have thought? His ma, at the kitchen sink, doing the dishes, holding up a bowl to the light to see if it was clean.

At the station he was put in a room. They told him they were waiting for his dad. He needed to be there before they could ask him any questions. They hadn't realised his age, that he was under eighteen. It smelled like the changing rooms in school in the room. They all knew his name, Barry this, Barry that. Then they took him through to another room where his dad was sitting, now wearing a suit. An eternity ago, his dad had got up to answer the door, only maybe forty minutes ago, and now here he was at a police station wearing a suit he never usually wore. Stapled on the cuff there was still the dry cleaner's pink paper after the previous time. The woman on the other side of the desk thanked his dad for coming.

Barry, she said. Do you want a coffee?

He said yes even though he had never drunk a coffee before. He needn't have worried because the coffee didn't ever come anyway.

She explained that they would need to record the interview and then a door opened and another man came in.

So, she said we need to ask you a few questions. And you've come here voluntarily. We need to ask you about a girl who's gone missing. Young girl of eight by the name of Megan Nichols. Now, Barry, have a look at this please. I am showing Barry a photo of Megan Nichols.

Looked straight off the mantelpiece, still in the brown cardboard frame of the annual school photo. She was wearing the same primary school uniform that he wore himself when he was a kid.

Do you know Megan Nichols? the woman asked.

Yeah, she's a kid I saw today, Barry said. She's a kid that I saw, I saw her today, but I don't know her. So, no, I don't know her.

She's gone missing, the woman said. Every parent's worst nightmare. Can you imagine?

No, said Barry. I mean, yes I can.

But you saw her?

I saw her in the park. In the kids' playground. The old one near the way in.

The kids' playground, the woman said. Alright. Would you have any idea what time that was at?

Maybe a bit after four, Barry said.

The woman leaned back in her seat.

And where exactly were you when you saw her? she asked.

I was in the kids' playground.

You were in a kids' playground?

No I went into the playground because I saw her there.

Barry swallowed hard.

You spoke to her?

Yeah.

Why were you speaking to this little girl, Barry?

He felt his dad turn slightly to listen to his answer.

She shouted at me to come over because she was stuck on a climbing frame. She was crying and she was stuck.

Yes, we know you spoke to her. You were seen speaking to her. Speaking to Megan Nichols.

There was a knock at the door and the woman left the table and then the room.

Dad, I'm sorry, Barry whispered, I don't know what's happening here, I've done nothing wrong at all.

Nothing wrong at all, years ago now, years ago, and so much in between. He cuts through the orange ties on another delivery that is stamped This Way Up. All the cardboard cut, all the items restocked, the notes taken, the cards read, receipts given, marking the distance between now and then. Displays rearranged, the garden furniture and the barbecues, wood-burning stoves with their artificial in-store fires, Christmas trees and the year's new toys, engagement rings under glass, wedding rings under glass, things put in bags, things pulled out of bags, times stepping onto the bus, times stepping off the bus. Washing your clothes, drying your clothes, getting them dirty again.

The woman came back in, apologetic. The guy looked at her and she nodded.

So, the woman said, you say that Megan Nichols was stuck.

I got her down from the climbing frame. She was stuck on the climbing frame.

So why couldn't she just get down herself?

Because she was stuck. I had to get her down.

How, stuck?

Her knickers were caught.

The word hovered somewhere above the table.

Her pants, he said. They were caught on the frame. That's why she couldn't get down.

The woman leaned in a little. Did you touch her pants, her underwear, Barry? Did you touch her pants?

The guy coughed and put his head down.

I couldn't not have touched them when I was trying to get her down from the frame. She was hooked on by her pants.

The woman said, You couldn't not have touched her pants.

No.

You just said that you couldn't not have touched her pants?

To get her down! Barry said. For Christ's sake. I'm trying to tell you she was stuck on the climbing frame, the other ones had wedgied her there and I got her down. There was nothing funny about it.

And it was all being faithfully recorded.

The woman said, That was the only physical contact you had with her?

Yes, said Barry. It wasn't really physical contact though, that sounds bad, it was like, three seconds, getting her down.

And you're sure about that?

Yeah, I'm sure about that, Barry said. Totally sure.

We're asking questions because a child is missing, the man said.

So after you touched her underwear, the woman said, what happened then? When she was down on the ground? What happened, Barry?

I, and he didn't want to say it, I gave her some money.

What did you do?

I gave her some money.

A child you didn't know? Why would you give a child you didn't know money?

Because she was upset! Because she was by herself and her friends had left her and she was upset and crying. 50p to buy an ice cream or a can of Coke and then that was it, she went off and I didn't see her again and that is all I can tell you.

The woman sat back on her seat. Fact remains though, Barry, she said, fact remains that you seem to be the last person to have seen this girl. Look at her photo again, Barry. Look at Megan Nichols' picture and let's start all over again.

Barry's dad spoke up then. He's told you, he said. He's told you what happened. Can I just check, is Barry under arrest or what is the situation here?

We're just asking him a few questions. He's come along voluntarily. To answer a few questions.

Her gaze was steady. So, she said, thank you very much.

We're meant to have a solicitor. We're meant to have someone else here, his dad said. Look at the state of him.

He hadn't realised that he had been working his skin, that his neck was up in weals. The crooks of his arms were on the point of bleeding.

What are you doing that for? the man said. Why's he doing that?

Stop doing that, the woman said.

She said they would take a break. Barry and his dad were shown through to a waiting room off where the main desk was. There was a man in a corner with the dregs of a black eye looking at his hands, one and then the other.

This is some to-do, his dad said. Some to-do indeed. I don't know solicitors. I've no dealings with solicitors. The only solicitor is the one we had to go to when your granny died and we were selling the house. It was a man in Carrick. He wouldn't know what to do here. He's all to do with selling houses. Selling houses and wills.

Barry wondered if he'd go to jail. It didn't matter if they hadn't done anything, sometimes people still ended up in jail.

Another policeman came through with a blue tub. Maybe you want to try putting that on, he said. She sent it to you. Our boss.

Should I put this on? Barry said.

If you think it'll do any good, his dad said. Stop that scrabbing.

There was thick silver paper on top of it and underneath gluey cream.

The perfume of it seemed to be everywhere in the waiting room. Did the guy with the black eye look over because he could smell it?

Barry felt he should put it on. The woman would maybe be angry if she came back and he hadn't put it on. That sort of stuff was pointless though. It was for women's faces. It wasn't medical. It clung to his fingers and he knew it would do no good, but he put it on one arm and then the other.

You won't be going to that park again, his dad said. There's always bad sorts around that park. Around all parks. What's keeping your woman? They'll be bringing us a solicitor now, no doubt. You'll have done nothing wrong, son, I know that. I know that. The solicitor will get it all sorted out. He looked around. Should I speak to somebody about the solicitor?

I don't know.

You hadn't even ever seen the wee girl before, sure you hadn't? No? Well, there you go.

No.

Her parents'll be beside themselves, he said. Bad people about.

There was the end of that film where a young fella in jail slits his wrists lying in his bed and you see the blood come seeping through the sheet.

The woman reappeared. She was looking different. Could she see he'd put on the cream? Was she happy because he'd used the cream?

We're letting you go, Barry, she said. There's a sighting of Megan Nichols just shortly after she left the park.

Barry handed her the tub of cream.

But that's not to say we won't need to speak to you again.

You understand that?

Barry had nothing to do with anything, his dad said.

His ma rushed down the stairs when they came into the house. His dad put his hand up and shook his head.

But what's happening? Don't go upstairs yet, Barry, his ma said. I'm just straightening out your room. Nearly finished.

The police had been round. They had gone to Barry's room to remove some stuff. Although what were they going to find, his ma said, other than dirty socks and pants? Isn't that right, Barry? You've not done anything wrong, have you? There was a police van outside. Mortifying, his ma said, them carrying stuff out. Never anybody on this road, but suddenly there's a whole bunch, all gawping.

The next day was a Saturday, but there was still no sign of Megan Nichols, nor on the Sunday either. She moved up the order of the headlines on the news. Megan Nichols' mother was on the screen, her two dark-eyed boys beside her. People in the neighbourhood arranged searches, posted flyers through doors. But no one came to Barry's house. When his dad went for the paper on Sunday morning, all talk stopped when he went into the shop. Barry knew what they would be saying. You see the bags came out of the house? Heard the polis held him for hours. No smoke without fire. Right odd-looking bloke, that fella, you'll have seen him about. Big guy with the skin. Don't judge a book by its cover, yeah I know, but even so. You heard about them taking anybody else in? No. No smoke without fire.

They were eating their dinner that night when the radio said that Megan Nichols was still missing. Poor wee pet, his ma said. Barry's dad got up. He said he thought he heard something out the front. What he saw was an egg running down the window. And then Barry and his ma were there too, watching one egg and then another. This was followed by showers of what sounded like gravel. Handful after handful.

Should I call the police? his mum asked.

No, said his dad. Don't do that.

On the Monday morning Megan Nichols was discovered. She was found by the caretaker opening up the primary school for the couple of teachers who liked to come in at the start of the summer to tidy up their rooms. Megan had spent the weekend eating old packets of biscuits left by teachers in the cupboard in the staffroom. There was a whole box of crisps too, from the end-of-year disco. Megan said she played with the school tortoise and messed about with the paints. She'd gone in to the school because she thought she'd seen Mrs Foster's car and she wanted to say have a nice summer to Mrs Foster who'd been absent on the last day. But she couldn't find Mrs Foster and then the place got locked up. Why didn't you use the phone in the staff room to ring for help? the woman on the telly asked her when she was briefly interviewed. She paused. I was liking the peace and quiet, she said. For a while that was a joke with people. If you wanted to take yourself off for some peace and quiet, you were doing a Megan Nichols.

Barry's mum was out that morning, brisk and efficient, dealing with the eggs like it was nothing other than a spring clean. There was paint on the front door, pale green, the colour somebody might have used for a bathroom. His da had to go to the DIY place to get the remover for it. It was decided that Barry would go to stay on the other side of town with an old uncle of his dad's. It was only ever presented as a temporary arrangement because sure didn't everyone know that Barry had done nothing wrong anyway? The uncle ate pies that came in tins and listened to the cricket on the radio. Barry lasted a year in the old uncle's place until he moved out, first into a damp old house with some others and then, when he got the job in this place, into the flat. And now he meets up with his parents in the town every few weeks or so, somewhere that does a business lunch or an early-bird meal because that's what they like. They've started getting vouchers that they print off the internet, complicated arrangements involving arriving and leaving restaurants at certain times. They've been to his flat, but they'd rather meet in the town. He goes back home for Christmas and that's alright because with the lights and the decorations and the empty streets on Christmas morning it feels like a different place. He always leaves in the afternoon. Can't hang about too long. Always working Boxing Day. Just the way the rota always seems to work out. His dad gives him a lift.

Phil comes through from the front of the shop. Barry, he says. Barry, you wouldn't come out here, would you? Only going to take a minute.

Barry puts down the blade and folds up the packing slips that he's laid out on the floor. They'll be coming again soon, the two of them, into the town for a meal. They'll ask about work. They'll ask about the flat. He'll say everything's alright, because it isn't that bad.

Glitch in the system, Phil says.

And where's James our manager? asks Barry.

Don't know, says Phil. Nipped out a couple of minutes ago. Said something about wanting to buy a shirt. Needs a white shirt. Got an interview for somewhere else this afternoon, I think. Some amount of managers running through this place, him, that other guy, the fat fella, Annie—

Yeah, Barry says. I know. Just the way it is.

Aye, so, two people have paid for the same item at exactly the same time, Phil explains. But there's only the one of the items actually in stock.

What they looking for?

Paint.

House paint?

Johnstone's Matt Emulsion in Cadillac.

You tried seeing if it's in the other shop?

Yeah, course I have, says Phil. But nah, no luck.

Okay, says Barry. Well there you go. They'll have to decide between them who gets it.

Well they both want it.

That's as may be, but if there's only the one tin.

Oh, Barry, you go and speak to them, Phil says. You're good at all that sort of stuff.

Yeah right, Barry says.

You are, Phil says. No messing. You got the knack.

Okay, okay, Barry sighs. And he goes out to the front to deal with the customers who are both holding their receipts for Johnstone's Matt Emulsion in Cadillac.

# Acknowledgements

Without Declan Meade and Sean O'Reilly this book and these stories would not exist. My debt to them is enormous.

Huge thanks to:

Lucy Luck at C+W, and to the editors of the various publications where some of these stories have appeared: Thomas Morris, Dawn Sherratt-Bado, Linda Anderson, Ian Maleney, and Sally Rooney; Lucy Caldwell; Michael Erskine; Robert Erskine; the Reid family.

My love to Bobby, Matilda, and my husband Paul, who graciously put up with me staring into the middle distance at the kitchen table as I pondered whether 'Would you gimme that?' was better than 'Gimme that would you?' You've all been so patient. Love too to Niamh Reid, and to the inspirational Rosemary Erskine, who hates bad language but appreciates these stories. Most of all, love and gratitude to the fine man and father, J B A Erskine, who did not live to see the publication of *Sweet Home*.